HAIR, SHE BEARS

USA TODAY BESTSELLING AUTHOR

ALYSSA DRAKE

For more information on Alyssa, please visit her website Alyssa Drake Novels or sign up for her newsletter, Love Notes, delivered directly to your inbox.

Summary: Missing since age five, a young woman discovers her captor never intended to release her, and reacts with a hasty plan which results in an unforeseen death.

Cover design by Covers by Combs
Editing by Personal Touch Editing
www.alyssadrakenovels.com

Candles flickered in the darkness of early morning, their faint light dancing across a faded patchwork quilt draped over the shoulders of a slight figure, hunched over a small wooden table. Her bare feet wrapped around the stem of the table, holding it to the floor while her shoulders moved back and forth as if rowing a bow. With each stroke, a soft scratching sound emanated from the stone cylinder she grasped with both hands.

Blisters coated her fingers, the result of hours of constant grinding. To her left, a wall of shelves, lined with racks of empty glass vials, waited for the deep purple powder forming on the giant mortar.

She straightened and dragged the side of her arm across her forehead, brushing away loose strands of hair. Her gaze dropped to a coil of golden hair, piled beside the small worktable. The hair snaked through the chamber, wound around a shabby paisley sofa, curved around to pass in front of a stone fireplace adorned with an austere rectangular mirror, then looped the room a second time before it crawled up the stairs toward her bedroom

—a trail of ennui. She sighed and leaned the pestle against the side of the stone bowl.

"Only one more ingredient." Her voice cracked, echoing in the empty tower. She rarely had occasion to speak as only one person ever visited her tower, but she found the quiet of early morning unsettling. When awake, as she often was at this time, she would speak to the mirror as if conversing with an old friend.

Rising, she cried out as pain shot through her legs and collapsed onto the stool, her soft gasps echoing off the high-raftered ceiling. The quilt dropped from her shoulders as she stamped her feet on the stone floor, willing the blood to flow through her stiff muscles. After a minute, she stood gingerly, stretched out one leg, pointing her toes, then flexed her foot. She repeated the process with the other leg, waiting until the prickling sensation eased before she hobbled toward a large window, the only source of natural light. She cupped her hands around her eyes and pressed her face against the wooden shutters, peering out through the slats. Soon, the sun would crest the surrounding mountains, bathing the tower with its warm kiss.

Shivering, she turned away and rubbed her hands over her bare arms, ignoring the tickle of a fallen tank top strap, a battle she gave up at some point after midnight. Truthfully, she would have worked shirtless, baggy clothing more of a hindrance than she cared to deal with, but she needed the warmth, and even clothing three sizes too large was better than nothing.

Her gaze shifted to the paltry fire sputtering in the fireplace. There was nothing left to burn unless she started on the sofa. Her eyes flicked to the mirror.

"Only if you're desperate," she said, her soft voice hitching. She bent over, collecting a section of hair from the floor.

Her hair.

"You must never cut more than you need." Mother's gruff voice rang from her memories, the comment accompanied by the sting

of a belt, punishment for a wasteful decision. *"You have less than ten minutes before the piece loses its magical properties."*

She winced, unconsciously rubbing her lower back, which still bore the scars of Mother's wrath. With that stringent rule in place, roughly thirty-five feet of blonde strands currently covered the living space, its growth aided by a tar-like concoction Mother forced her to swallow weekly.

Dropping the quilt to the floor, she methodically wound the hair around her arm like a rope as her gaze followed the river of gold up the staircase to a small loft, which held a four-posted bed hidden behind a ratty burgundy curtain. The bottom of her hair appeared on the top stair. It fluttered in the early morning breeze that snuck in through the slats of the giant shutters.

She hefted the coil of hair onto her shoulder and trudged over to the staircase, panting from the weight. Dropping the hair on the bottom step, she leaned forward, grasped the section trailing up the stairs, and yanked it toward her.

If twenty vials of powder required one inch of hair, then fifty vials meant two-and-a-half... she measured the strands with her palm. Her hand slid down over her hip, dipped under the hem of her shirt, and wrapped around the knife strapped to her thigh. With a quick flick, she ripped the knife from the leather sheath and slashed it across her hair. The stands came away easily.

She shoved the knife back into the sheath and returned to the small table by way of the fireplace—one final burst of warmth before she returned to her task. She bent to snag the quilt from the floor and cried out as a sharp pain flashed across the back of her head. Without turning, she reached behind her, grasped her hair—stretched taut like a golden tightrope—and jerked, freeing her hair from the sofa leg. Rolling her eyes, she sank back onto the stool, massaging her scalp.

"Maybe I should burn you," she said to her hair, knowing the threat was futile. Mother's wrath was far worse than freezing in an empty tower.

Setting the strands of hair on the side of the mortar, she rolled her head back and forth, loosening her shoulders, and extracted the knife again. She passed the knife over the ends, slicing off a small section, and sprinkled the pieces over the mortar. Repeating the action, she carved the hair into miniscule pieces, then returned the knife to her thigh, lifted the pestle, and resumed grinding.

No sound reverberated in the room except the soft scraping of stone on stone. After ten minutes, one hand felt along the side of the table and closed around a small silver spoon, which hung from a miniscule hook. Lifting the spoon, she scraped it along the sides of the mortar, mixing in the residue and grinding it with the pestle. When the lavender powder darkened to royal purple, she set the pestle and spoon down, a sigh of relief escaping her lips.

Reaching to her left, she grabbed the nearest vial from the shelf, uncorked the top, placed the plug in her lap, and held the bottle over the mortar. She dipped the spoon into the mixture and tapping the edge of the spoon with her pinkie, filled the vial three-quarters full. After retrieving the cork from her lap, she shoved the stopper into the bottle. Holding the vial in one of the sunbeams streaming through the shutters, she shook it. Light struck the glass bottle, casting purple sparkles across the floor.

"Never a full dose." Mother's voice growled, his fury swirled around her. *"We don't want to cure them, just give them a taste of possibility."*

Votras Alute, the magical powder peddled by Mother's crew, promised to ease a person's pain instantly. However, by restricting the dosage, Mother prevented the person from receiving permanent relief, and within a few days, they were begging for another delivery.

"In this world, the big take from the small," Mother said. *"It is nature."*

"It's wrong," her young voice had replied, earning Mother's ire and five lashes from the belt. As additional punishment for her sympathy, Mother refused to bring food for one week.

She shuddered, her stomach rumbling at the recollection. Her gaze flicked to the loose stone at the base of the staircase. Hidden beneath it was a small cache of food and a silver necklace, the one she had been wearing when Mother kidnapped her.

Rising, she set the mostly full vial back on the shelf, covered the mortar with a cloth, and walked over to the staircase. She knelt, wincing as the stones bit into her knees, and pushed the coil of hair aside. Digging her fingernails under the edge of a stone, she pulled it free of the floor and placed it on the first step.

The silver necklace glowed in the dim cache. She reached down and extracted it from the hole. Holding it up to her throat, she shivered as the cold metal touched her skin.

On her tenth birthday, Mother tried to confiscate the necklace as payment for a subpar batch, but Zenna told him she had lost it. He beat her severely for her negligence and threatened to throw her from the tower. She spent days in agony, bruised head to toe, but the punishment was worth it. The necklace was the only memento of her life before Mother.

She fastened the necklace around her throat, her fingers finding the small heart charm which hung in the center. Tucking the charm underneath her shirt, she walked to the window and pushed the shutters open.

The cool breeze rushed forward to greet her. Her eyes slid over the horizon, finding the sun as it peeked over the high mountains surrounding the valley. The quilt slid from her shoulders. Stepping onto the window ledge, she reached up and grabbed the eaves. With a grunt, she pulled herself through the window, climbed onto the roof, and crawled to the top of the tower. After wrapping her fingers through the spire, she turned and faced the sunrise. Closing her eyes, she inhaled as the sun painted her face with warmth.

Mother had forbidden her from leaving the compound until

her parents' debt was cleared. However, Mother never said she couldn't leave the tower... not that Mother was aware she was up here. She inhaled again, enjoying the crisp feel of the wind blowing across her face.

"Don't jump!"

She started and grabbed hold of the spire with both hands to prevent herself from falling. Glaring over the edge of the roof, her gaze sought the origin of the voice. A tiny speck dashed across the courtyard and skidded to a halt at the base of the tower, one of four which rose out of the compound like giant stone sentries.

"Don't jump!" The voice yelled again, the deep rumble reminding her of Mother's gruff tone.

She tightened her grip on the spire and leaned forward. Cupping her hand around her mouth, she yelled back, praying Mother would not hear her. "I'm not going to jump."

"Then, what the hell are you doing?" the man asked, dashing back and forth beneath her as if he intended to catch her.

"I'm watching the sunrise."

"You could do that on the ground." He stopped running and stepped back, keeping his arms outstretched.

Mother was going to hear of this, and the punishment would be severe. Zenna bit her lip and crouched down. Scooting down the roof, she straddled the gable and leaned over the side.

"Why are you awake?" she asked.

"That's your question?" An audible choking sound rose from the ground. "You're on a roof!"

"And I am perfectly safe."

"Not from where I'm standing." The man folded his arms across his chest.

Grimacing, she slid her leg over the side of the roof, wrapped her fingers around the shingles, and swung back through the window, landing on the floor with a soft grunt, and spun around.

"Satisfied?" she asked, peering down.

"Yes, thank you." He took a step closer.

She licked her lips. "Please don't tell Mother you saw me on the roof."

"Tell me your name," he said, a forceful undertone to his command.

"Swear not to reveal to Mother where you found me." She placed her hands on the windowsill and leaned out further. "Do I have your word?"

"I swear," he replied, his voice laced with amusement, and held up his right hand.

"My name is Zenna."

"Zenna." He spread his arms out wide and bowed. "It is a pleasure to meet you, my name is Malik."

Malik? As in Mother's son? Her heart stopped, a corset of fear crushing her chest.

"I-I-I thought Malik controlled the territory to the north."

"I do."

"Then why are you here?" she asked, a tremor rippled through her body. She would never see daylight again.

"My presence was requested." He thumbed over his shoulder at the compound. "All the captains will be here this morning."

"Why?"

Malik twisted away from her question—curiosity was never encouraged by Mother. She cringed, waiting for Malik's castigation. After a moment of silence, he returned his gaze to her.

"If I knew, I wouldn't be here."

"I doubt that," Zenna replied.

He snorted. "Will you be attending?"

"She's not invited." The air beside Malik shimmered, and Mother materialized.

"Good morning, Father," Malik said, his demeanor unaffected by Mother's sudden appearance.

Mac "Mother" Gothel had taken control of the city roughly twenty years ago. His father, a longtime driver for the Rossi family, sent his son to college to deter him from criminal pursuits. Instead, Mother used his botanical education to invent Votras Alute, a healing powder which based its formula around a rare purple flower he discovered while trekking through the rainforests. He brought a prototype to Bruno, the head of the Rossi family. However, due to the flower's inaccessible location, the drug was rejected, and Mother was responsible for the bullet, which took Bruno's life.

"I specifically remember telling you to stay away from the south tower," Mother said, his gaze locked on Zenna.

"You told me the south tower was empty," Malik replied.

"It is."

"Clearly, it is not." Malik gestured at Zenna, who had ducked down and was peering at them over the edge of the windowsill.

"Zenna!" Mother's annoyance whipped up the side of the tower. She popped up, her heart thudded.

"Good morning, Mother," she said, her voice falsely bright.

"Before I beat you unconscious, explain why my son is standing beneath your window."

Zenna trembled. Her eyes flicked to Malik. Would he lie for her? If she admitted she was on the roof, Mother would seal the window shut. Zenna took a deep breath.

"I was working on a new batch, and there wasn't enough light in the tower, so I leaned out the window to check the color in the sunlight."

"A new batch?" A cold smile broke Mother's fury, and he rubbed his hands together. "This is excellent timing. How does it look?"

"What the hell?" Malik asked, interrupting Zenna's response.

Mother turned to him. Zenna could not see Mother's face, but she did catch Malik's flinch.

"Would you care to rephrase that?" Mother folded his arms across his broad chest.

"You have some poor girl chained up in a tower,"—he slashed

his hand toward Zenna—"and you're forcing her to manufacture Votras Alute?"

"She's not chained up."

"Prove it." Malik folded his arms, mirroring his father's stance. Silence stretched between them, neither of them moved, then Mother laughed, his deep voice winding around the tower.

"No doubt, you are my son." He clapped Malik on the back and ruffled his long hair in an affectionate gesture Zenna would have sworn was impossible for Mother to exhibit. "You are correct, the south tower is not abandoned."

"How long has she been here?" Malik jerked his head toward Zenna.

"Most of her life," replied Mother, his voice holding no sympathy. "There's only one entrance."

Mother waved his hand, he and Malik vanished like wisps of smoke, and Mother reappeared beside Zenna. She screamed and stepped back toward the window, tripping over her hair. Hands flailing, she stumbled, unable to regain her balance, and crashed into a solid mass.

"Careful now," Malik said, his rumbled warning causing her stomach to flip over. "Wouldn't want you to fall out the window."

Her heart pounded, inspired by his seductive voice. He wound an arm around her waist, steadying her. She lifted her gaze, stared into his icy-blue eyes, and her breath caught. She had never been this close to a man before, except for Mother. Her gaze roved over Malik, drinking in his unruly chestnut brown hair, broad chest—akin to his father's—and unnerving eyes. She swallowed, her tongue stuck to the roof of her mouth.

Mother's iron grip closed around Zenna's wrist and yanked her from Malik's embrace, dragging her across the floor, and flung her at the small table.

"Bring me a bottle."

Nodding, Zenna hastened to the shelf, removed the filled vial, and spun around. Mother's dark gaze slid down her shirt and stopped at the short hem brushing her thighs.

"That's an interesting outfit." He took a step forward. Zenna copied his movement, scooting backward, and knocked her elbow against the shelf.

"It's too big," she said and blushed, tugging at the hem.

Mother snapped his fingers and opened his palm. She stretched out her arm, offering the vial to him. As soon as the bottle left her hand, she scuttled around her worktable, placing it between her and Mother.

"You just made this?" he asked, lifting the vial even with his eye and tapping the side.

She nodded, her attention flicking to Malik. He stood immobile, his hands clasped in front of his waist, a younger version of Mother—leather vest, worn jeans, heavy boots, and an unspoken aura of danger, which circled them both like black clouds. Malik tilted his head, and his gaze skated over her, hovering on the exposed swell of her breasts. Heat rose to her cheeks, and she tore her eyes from him.

Uncorking the top, Mother tipped the vial, and tapped a pinch of the purple powder into his hand, touched the tip of his tongue to the powder, then closed his eyes. After a minute, he opened them—they glowed black.

"This is one of your better ones." He turned away and held the bottle out to Malik. "Test it."

"I don't use Votras Alute." Malik shook his head and held up his hands, stepping backward.

"Why?" Mother frowned. "You sell it. You should know what it does to the body."

"I know how it feels, and I have no need for it," Malik replied, setting his feet. "I'm healthy."

"I said to try it." Mother's eyes narrowed, and a low snarl grew in his throat.

Malik snatched the vial from his father and held it up. With his tongue trapped between his teeth, he shook the glittering powder, then shifted his gaze to Zenna.

"You're correct, there is not enough light in here."

Mother's face purpled.

A tiny grin passed over Malik's face, and Zenna was certain she saw him wink. With a sigh, he tilted the vial, tapping a tiny portion into his palm. Raising his eyes to his father, he licked his hand, shivering as the powder released into his body.

"Better?" Mother asked, his coal eyes blazed as he retrieved the vial from Malik, sealed it, and slipped it into his breast pocket.

"No." Malik's tongue garbled the word. His unfocused gaze sliding over the room, he stumbled, moving toward the sofa, and collapsed with a grunt, dropping his head into his hands. "I need to sit."

"You wouldn't have that reaction if you consistently used Votras Alute." Mother threaded his beefy fingers through Malik's shaggy hair and yanked his head up, wrenching it until Malik stared into his eyes. "I need my soldiers to be strong, especially you. I expect you to ingest one serving each day."

"And if I refuse?" Malik asked, his eyes rolling.

"What happens to people who refuse me?" Mother lifted his gaze to Zenna.

"You kill them." Just like he threatened to kill Zenna's parents if she refused to create the drug for him.

"Exactly." Mother laughed, the cruel sound sending ice sliding down Zenna's spine, and flung Malik off the sofa toward the open window. His inhuman strength was a side effect of consistent use of Votras Alute.

Zenna screamed as Malik crashed into the wall, less than a foot away from the opening. He dropped to the stone floor, his limbs folded beneath him, groans poured from his mouth. She dashed across the room but froze beside the sofa when Mother held up his hand as he strode to Malik's writhing body.

"If you were anyone else but my son, I would have thrown you out the window." Kneeling, Mother wrapped his fingers through Malik's hair again and jerked his head from the floor. Blood trickled from the corner of Malik's mouth. Mother leaned closer, dropping his voice to a low growl. "The next time you defy me, I will kill you. Do I make myself clear?"

"Yes," Malik replied through clenched teeth. He wiped the back of his hand across his chin, smearing the blood.

"Good." Mother glanced over his shoulder at Zenna, his eyebrows pulled together into a scowl. "What is that?"

"What?" Zenna stepped backward. Her hand flew to her chest, and the necklace hidden beneath her shirt.

"That. You told me you lost that." One thick finger pointed at the heart-shaped bulge. His voice dropped to a menacing growl. "Did you lie to me?"

2

"I found it this morning." Zenna trembled as Mother advanced. His hand whipped out and closed around her upper arm, jerking her to him. Reaching under her hair, his jagged fingernails scratching her skin, he unfastened the necklace and pulled it from her throat. His fingers curled around the small heart, crushing it in his hand.

"I expect every vial to be filled by the time I return this afternoon." He shook his fist under her nose. "You know the consequences of failure."

Pain was Mother's favorite punishment.

Zenna nodded, unable to speak. Her gaze followed Mother's hand and the silver chain spilling over his fingers. How could she have been so careless? Mother had stripped every happy memory from her.

"You are expected at the meeting this afternoon, Malik. Clean yourself up." Mother waved his hand and disappeared.

"That went better than expected." With a moan, Malik flipped over to his back and stared at the ceiling, his laborious breathing the only sound in the tower.

"Can I help you?" Zenna asked, edging closer.

"You can't even help yourself," Malik snorted. His head lolled toward her. "How do you propose to help me?"

"It seemed like the thing to say." Zenna shrugged and retrieved a clean tank top from an armoire at the base of the staircase. Spinning around, she took one small step toward Malik. "I don't get much company."

"I suppose you don't." Sitting up, Malik hissed and touched his finger to the corner of his mouth. Blood came away on the tip.

"Take this." Inching closer, Zenna held out the shirt. He reached over and grasped the cloth. Zenna darted away from him, leaving the tank top dangling from his fingers.

"This looks like one of mine." Crumpling the shirt in his fist, he chuckled to himself and leaned back against the wall, pressing it to his mouth with a wince. "How did you end up here?"

"I am repaying a debt." Zenna snatched the quilt from the floor and wrapped it over her shoulders, then sat on the far end of the sofa, eyeing him with curiosity and a touch of fear.

"A lifetime is a hefty debt." He removed the shirt, refolded it, and placed the clean side against his lip, a groan accompanying his movement.

"I've almost paid it back." She tucked the quilt over her legs, shoving the edges underneath her thighs.

"Is my father aware of that?" Malik asked through closed eyes.

"I have recorded everything." She indicated a small leather-bound journal beneath the shelves of vials with a jerk of her head. "He cannot deny me."

"How much was the original debt?"

"Four hundred thousand."

He whistled, his eyes opening. "That's quite a large amount."

"It was my parents' debt. When my mother was pregnant with me, she fell gravely ill. My father was so desperate to save her life, he made a costly error. After I was born, Mother came to collect, and my father couldn't pay." Her voice trailed off. She picked at a loose thread on the quilt.

"When did he take you?" His gentle tone caused her to glance up.

"I was five."

Malik rose with a groan and stumbled backward, steadying himself against the wall. He gagged, pressed his hand to his mouth, and inhaled a deep breath.

"Have you ever used Votras Alute?" he asked, his tongue thick.

"Once."

"Only once?" Malik shoved off the wall, lumbered across the room, his gait akin to a drunkard, and collapsed beside her. Leaning his head against the back of the sofa, his eyes fluttered closed again. The heavy aroma of petrol and leather assaulted her.

"It doesn't work for me... because of the secret ingredient."

"I thought it was a plant."

"Mother changed the recipe."

"What is it now?" He opened his eyes and turned his penetrating icy-blue gaze on her.

Zenna swallowed. If Mother didn't trust Malik with the formula, should she? She had no experience with Malik and could only draw from rumors, hushed conversations that drifted up from the courtyard from the mouths of men too terrified to confront Mother's son.

"I..."

"You can't say?"

She licked her lips. "If I tell you..."

"I swear not to say one word to my father." He lifted his hand and slapped it over his heart, offering her a half-grin.

"As he and I are the only people who know, it wouldn't be difficult for him to figure out who told you."

"And you think I'll steal the formula and manufacture it myself?"

"Not exactly." Zenna wound her fingers together and glanced

over her shoulder at the shelf of empty vials. "But you might kidnap me."

Malik's unusual scent intensified as he moved closer. Hooking his fingers under her chin, he dragged her face toward him, the pad of his thumb sliding across her lower lip, sending a tremor zipping through her body.

"And you believe my father is a better warden than I?" His soft question caressed her skin, a second shiver rippled down her spine.

"I don't know you. I can't trust you."

"You can't trust my father, either," Malik replied. He twisted around, hung the blood-stained shirt over the edge of the sofa, and turned back to her with a half-smile. "What would put your mind at ease?"

"A kiss." The words burst from her lips before she could stop them.

Malik paused, clearly thrown by her request, and peculiar expression washed over his face.

"You do know who I am?"

She dropped her gaze, her fingers winding together in her lap, and the edges of the quilt pulled apart. This was the stupidest idea she'd ever had, but she could think of only one way to prevent Malik from revealing he knew the formula, and that was to put his own life at risk. He didn't need to know he would be her first kiss. A strange ache to spread through her chest. What if he thought her ridiculous?

"Mother will kill you if he learns you kissed me," Zenna said to the floor. "This way, I have your silence."

"Aren't you a smart one?" Malik laughed, the delightful baritone sound rumbling around the tower. "Alright, you have a deal."

Before Zenna could react, Malik leaned forward, lifted her chin, and pressed his mouth to hers. His arms wound around her waist, drawing her body against his solid chest. Increasing the pressure against her mouth, his lips parted hers, and his tongue dipped into her mouth. Her body felt as though it was aflame as if the heat from her skin would burn through her tank top and set them both on fire. She moaned, longing to drag her fingers through his hair.

Malik released her and moved back to the opposite side of the sofa, his bright eyes glowing with hunger. Zenna sucked in a shaky breath, trembling under the memory of Malik's sensual caress.

"I have put my life in jeopardy at your request. What is the secret ingredient?"

"Me."

"You?" Malik frowned.

Zenna gestured at the hair piled at the base of the staircase. He blinked several times, his gaze flicking between her and the pile of golden hair. He leaned forward and rubbed his forehead with his hand.

"Give me a moment, I'm trying to process what you said. This drug makes it impossible to think."

"Is that why you don't use it?" Zenna asked.

"Well that, and apparently, it's made from human hair!" He glanced up, anger darkening his features. "How long has your hair been in the formula?"

"Ever since I was taken." She scooted away from his ire and drawing her feet beneath her, pressed herself against the far end of the sofa. He reached out, his hand hovering just above her forearm. When she shrank away further, he retracted his arm with a sigh.

"I didn't mean to frighten you." He placed his hand on the sofa halfway between them.

"You look just like Mother when you're angry," she replied, glancing at his hand.

"I'm not him." His fingers tapped the sofa cushion.

"Your reputation claims otherwise."

"And how did you come by this damning information?" Malik

turned to his left and then his right in an exaggerated movement, drinking in the austere furniture in the tower. He stroked his chin as if contemplating her words. "Do you receive your gossip by carrier pigeon?"

She giggled, then clamped her hand over her mouth, her eyes rounding. "I apologize, I didn't mean to laugh."

"I don't mind." Leaning over, he reached out and placed one gentle finger on her hand. Lowering it from her mouth, he smiled. "It's not a sound I'm accustomed to."

"Your mother…" He flinched at the word, and she sank her teeth into her lip, stopping the question.

"Dead." Malik rose and trudged to the open window. Staring out at the courtyard, he slammed his palm flat on the right side of the wall. The sound startled Zenna, who leapt off the sofa, abandoning the quilt, and retreated behind her worktable. He glanced back, his face softening.

"I won't hurt you, I swear."

"Mother said the same thing the night he kidnapped me." Zenna shuffled forward two steps.

Malik pressed his lips together into a thin line. His gaze skated over the shelves. Crossing the room, he stopped in front of the worktable, then lifted the cloth from the mortar, staring at the deep purple powder.

"My father isn't going to let you leave."

"What do you mean?" Zenna's heart constricted. Mother had to let her go. This batch paid off the balance owed, there was no reason to keep her.

"Your hair is the key to Votras Alute. The whole operation depends upon the sale of that drug." Malik lifted his eyes.

"And you think Mother will renege on our agreement?" Zenna asked, despair seeping into her body. Tears gathered along her eyelashes.

"He had no intention of ever honoring it." Sighing, Malik stepped around the worktable and wrapped her in a hesitant embrace, brushing his lips across the top of her head. "I am sorry to be the one to tell you."

"Maybe you should kidnap me," Zenna said, muttering the words into his chest.

"I'm not any kinder," he replied and stepped back, a hard mask sliding over his face.

"So, you're not going to help me?" She sniffled, a sob stuck in her throat.

Malik shook his head.

"You're going to be late for your meeting, and I have a lot of work to do." Zenna turned away from him, rolling her shoulders back. Walking to the shelves lining the wall, she selected an empty vial from the top rack. He moved behind her and clasped her upper arms.

"Mother would kill us both if I took you."

Zenna stiffened. "You need to leave."

"I can't." Malik gestured around the tower. "There's no door."

"But Mother—"

"Has abilities which I do not," he interrupted with a snarl. "For someone who claims to know my reputation, you got that part wrong."

"Then how are you supposed to attend the meeting?" A wrinkle carved into her forehead, she spun around, her eyes searching his.

"That's part of my punishment." Malik twisted away from her probing gaze and returned to the window. Leaning out, he stared down at the tufts of grass shoving through the stones surrounding the base of the tower. "If I'm late…"

"What would your father do in your position?" she asked, setting the empty vial beside the mortar.

"He'd take the powder and jump from the window."

"It's over forty feet!"

"How do you know that?" Malik glanced back at her.

She blushed, indicating the trail of golden hair. "Mother requires me to record the length every week."

"And you have occasion to hang your hair out the window?"

"It gets in the way when I'm working." She sank down on the stool and lifted the metal spoon, which she scraped along the bottom of the mortar. Picking up the vial, she tapped the edge of the spoon, filling the vial with the powder. Malik appeared beside her and took the vial from her hand. She turned, a protest on her lips.

"I can only think of two ways out of this tower," he said, speaking more to the glittering powder than to her.

"Please don't jump!" The spoon clinked against the side of the mortar as Zenna leapt off the stool and grabbed his arm. His bicep flexed underneath her fingers.

"Would you miss me?" Amusement flashed across his hardened features. "Did you not just throw me out?"

"Since my abduction, I have met no other person, save your father." She licked her lips. "You are an improvement."

"I'm not the best company, either." Malik turned away, set the filled vial into a rack on the top shelf, removed the empty one next to it, and passed it to Zenna.

"What is your other option?" she asked, accepting the bottle.

"You." His hand closed around a strand of hair, rubbing it between his fingers, then his gaze slid to the window. "I'll cut your hair and use it as a rope."

"You can't!" She jerked away and crashed into the table, which scraped backward across the floor and slammed into the wall. The stool rolled in the opposite direction, smacking into the sofa. Her hand dropped to her side, ducked under the hem of her shirt, and ripped the knife from the sheath. She brandished it, the blade glinting in the sunlight. The defensive movement brought a scowl to Malik's lips.

"Are you going to fight me?" He moved closer, trapping her between his body and the table. One hand closed around her wrist and wrenched it sideways until she cried out, and the knife clattered to the floor.

"I accept that you have no intention of saving me from my debt, but I beg you, please don't cause my death." She cringed, praying Malik's fists were not as painful as Mother's.

"How would cutting your hair kill you?" He released her wrist, and his arms shot forward, smashing into the wall behind her. Leaning forward, he forced her to contort backward into an unnatural arc. She grabbed the sides of the table, her fingers curling around the edges. The bright blue of his eyes darkened to black, a frightening mirror of his father.

"Don't lie to me," he snarled.

She dragged in a breath, her chest barely rising before it pressed against his. She wanted to look away, but she froze, her heart hammering a violent rhythm of fear. She knew he could feel it, watching as the realization passed through his eyes. His mouth curved into a dark smile as he bent closer, pressing himself into her.

"Once cut, the hair loses its potency. You would cost Mother thousands." As the words spilled from her mouth, her lips brushed against his.

"How long before it's useless?"

His whispered question sent tingles skating across her lower lip as his mouth caressed hers. Her stomach flipped over, and an overwhelming desire to touch him surfaced in the dark recesses of her mind—like lightning coursing through her body.

"Ten minutes."

One hand betrayed her, releasing its hold on the table, and skated over his skin, starting at the pulsating sinew of his forearm, and moving to the inside portion of his elbow. As her fingers reached his shoulder, he growled, his mouth pressing roughly against hers. Thrusting past her lips, his tongue teased her, sending shivers cascading down her spine. His arms encircled her waist, yanking her body off the table, and secured it against his in one quick movement. He wrapped her legs around his hips and stumbled toward the sofa, his mouth never leaving hers. Her fingers slid into his hair as he collapsed on the sofa, drawing her onto his lap, and his mouth devoured hers.

"He should never have left me with you," Malik said as he broke the kiss, his mouth skated along her throat.

"Why?" She panted the word, gasping as Malik's teeth nipped at her ear.

"Because of my reputation…" He froze, cursed, then lifted Zenna from his lap. Setting her firmly on the cushion next to him, he cursed again.

"Did I do something wrong?" She drew her legs to her chest. Malik was her first kiss—and her second—but she knew, without any doubt, she was not his.

"No. I have to go." His frantic gaze jumped around the tower, landing on the filled vial. "May I have that?"

She nodded, unable to speak. He was abandoning her, leaving her to his father's wrath. She felt tears growing in the corners of her eyes and blinked rapidly to clear them.

"Zenna." He dropped to his knees in front of the sofa and sighed. "Don't you see, I can't stay? No good will come from our association."

"You'd rather take a drug, you loathe?" She glared at him.

His mouth twitched. He reached out, his hand hovering between them. When she did not turn away, he cupped the side of her face.

"I'd rather spend the night." He drew the side of his thumb down her cheek. "There are more firsts I'd like to experience with you."

Her mouth popped open. "You knew?"

"Of course." His baritone laughter reverberated through the tower again. "I didn't know you existed until this morning, how many other men could you have met during your imprisonment?"

"But you kissed me, anyway?"

"It was your request."

"Not the second time."

"The second time I wanted to." His eyes glowed.

"And now?"

"I still want to." His gaze dragged down her body. Extracting the vial from his pocket, he tapped the glass against his palm. "Mother won't kill you, he needs you, but I'm expendable, and I don't look forward to being thrown from this tower for tardiness, no matter how tempted I am to stay."

Uncorking the bottle, he tilted back his head, then upended the contents, his face contorting as the powder touched his tongue. He lowered his head and slumped over, the glass vial rolling from his twitching fingers.

"Malik!" Zenna dropped beside him. Sliding her hand underneath his head, she lifted it from the floor and cradled it in her lap. Her fingertips stroked across his sweat-covered forehead as his body jerked. He grabbed her hand, his fingers tightening until she cried out, and he opened his eyes.

"I'm fine." His tongue slurred the words. Releasing her wrist, he flipped onto his stomach, then pushed up onto his knees and crawled to the window.

"There has to be another way." Zenna trailed behind him, her fingers wound into knots. "You could die."

"Only if you made the batch wrong."

She bristled at his statement, indignant at the accusation.

"I haven't made a batch wrong since I was ten!"

"That's good to know." He hauled his body onto the windowsill, pulled himself up, and straddled the wood, hanging one foot outside the tower. His head swiveled toward her, a dark expression flickered over his face. "I hope he's watching."

Forcing a smile, he leaned sideways and fell out the window. Zenna screamed, dove for his hand, and missed, crashing into the windowsill, and doubled over at the waist with a grunt. Malik tumbled, head over feet, and landed flat on his back. An explosive curse word floated up from the ground.

"Are you alive?" Zenna asked, leaning out the window.

"I think so." Malik's faint reply barely reached her.

"Can you move?" she asked, unable to hide the worry in her voice.

"He'll be fine."

Zenna screamed and spun around. Mother stepped out from beneath the staircase, his eyes on the empty vials.

"They will be finished on time," she said, answering Mother's unasked question.

Nodding once, Mother ambled toward her, his dark glower locked on her face. When he reached the window, he stopped and peered out. Upon finding Malik, Mother grunted once and pulled his head back in, then turned to Zenna.

"I'm surprised he jumped. I would have thought you too enticing for him."

"I don't understand." Zenna twisted her fingers together.

Mother's hand whipped out, closed around Zenna's arm, and dragged her to him, his cigar-stained breath wrinkling her nose.

"An innocent," he replied, then laughed, his gruff bark a chilling contrast to Malik's warm baritone. He scraped his fingernail down her arm "You don't know my son's character, do you?"

"I assume he is like you," Zenna replied, wrenching her arm out of Mother's grasp.

"He's worse. He's developed quite a collection of women over his lifetime." A sneer hovered on Mother's lips. "Did he tell you he was engaged?"

3

"Engaged?" But he kissed her... twice! Numbness flooded her body. Her legs wobbling, she staggered to the sofa and dropped onto the cushion. The word buzzed around her head.

"Neglected to mention that, did he?" Mother strolled around the back of the sofa and stopped directly behind her. Locking eyes with her in the mirror, he clamped his hands on her shoulders, resting his bulk on her small frame. "Malik has never been one for honesty. Perhaps that is the reason he excels in this business."

"He..."

"Are you defending my son? One hour with him and suddenly, you are his champion. I shall have to ask him his secret." Mother's grip tightened, digging into Zenna's collarbones. "You didn't have sex with him, did you?"

"No!" Zenna attempted to jerk free, but Mother's iron grasp pinned her to the sofa.

Leaning down, he whispered in her ear. "Do you know what sex is?"

"I've read about it."

Mother ripped her over the back of the sofa and slammed her

against the wall, his fingers curled around her throat. Her feet swung above the floor, kicking madly as she clawed at his hand, gasping for oxygen.

"What have you been reading?" He lowered her just enough that her toes touched the cold stone.

"Only what you've brought me," she replied, her voice hoarse. Her eyes slid to the right, indicating a small shelf with several worn books, rare presents from Mother.

"I will have to choose more carefully in the future." Mother leaned forward, his body pressed against hers. "Were you intrigued? Would you like me to show you what sex feels like?"

She shook her head. "I don't believe I would find the experience enjoyable."

Mother snorted, released her, and vanished. She heard his voice in the courtyard below. "Next time, try not to land on your back."

"Fuck you," Malik replied, anguish accompanied his retort.

Mother's snicker rose to Zenna's window. She crept over and peered out. Malik lay immobile beneath the tower. Mother crouched beside him and extracted the vial from his pocket.

"I don't want any more."

"You need it." Forcing the bottle between Malik's teeth, Mother tapped the contents into Malik's mouth. He choked on the powder, but Mother covered Malik's mouth with his hand and rubbed his throat, forcing his son to swallow the drug.

"Disgusting," Malik's raspy voice announced once Mother removed his hand.

"And yet, now you can move."

"I wouldn't have needed it at all if you kept Zenna in a normal location." Malik sat up, his hands moving over his limbs as if checking for broken bones.

"Zenna? Are we on a first-name basis with the chemist?"

"She's a captive."

"She's a debtor." Rising, Mother offered his hand to Malik, who smacked it away and struggled to his feet.

"And what happens when she pays off the debt? Do you let her go?"

"Always so concerned with the less fortunate." Mother ruffled Malik's hair. "Your mother had the same unbearable trait."

"Is that why you killed her?" The hatred that flowed from Malik wound around the tower and crept in through the window.

"She betrayed us." Mother's hands clenched. "She was going to shut down the business, take you away from me, and send me to prison."

"That's where you belong." Malik's head turned toward the sound of engines revving in the distance; the territory bosses approached.

"As do you, my boy, or have you forgotten your role in our organization?" Mother clapped Malik in the center of the back.

"Your organization," Malik replied, his tone harsh.

"Don't you forget that little detail." Shoving Malik forward, Mother glanced back at the tower, his eyes locking with Zenna. He held up two fingers, indicating the time he would return.

Zenna nodded. She waited until they entered the main building in the center of the compound before retiring from the window and dragged to the shelves. No one was going to rescue her, not her parents, not Malik, not a knight in shining armor. She drew a finger across a row of empty vials, staring unseeingly at the shelves. She shook her head and glanced right, seeking the worktable, which remained shoved against the wall, testimony of her inability to resist Malik's charisma. A blush ripped through her skin at the memory of his mouth on her lips, his body pressed against her.

Engaged.

Mother's gruff voice swirled around her, and pain slash sliced through her chest. Crying out, she dropped to her knees. What had she expected from one kiss... true love? Malik was Mother's son, a byproduct of his cruel nature.

Her first memory of Malik—witnessed from her tower window—was of a boy, barely fourteen, kneeling silently before his father in the courtyard, flinching each time the whip crossed his bare back. Mother's ire rolled across the compound as he swung his arm in a relentless rhythm, beating Malik until he collapsed. Malik never made a sound and emerged from the encounter strong, violent, and pitiless. The rumors that followed, the whispered shock at the things he was capable of... Zenna shivered. The only man more dangerous than Malik was his father.

She wrestled the worktable back to its original position, then spun around, searching for the missing stool. It appeared beside the sofa, one leg wedged underneath the low frame. She tugged the stool free with a grunt, and set it upright, her gaze sliding to the window.

Mother had to let her go, he gave his word. Today's batch would be worth more than enough to clear her parents' obligation. *And if he refuses?* Malik's deep baritone echoed in her mind. She wanted to argue with him, but she feared he was correct. What would she do if Mother denied her?

She rose and lifted a shabby half-apron from a small hook beside the shelves. After wrapping the apron strings around her waist twice, she tied them in a square knot, collected ten bottles from the top row, and tucked them into the apron pocket. Retrieving the knife, she slipped the blade back into the sheath and sank onto the stool, her feet wrapping automatically around the table's stem. Rummaging in the apron, she retrieved a bottle and held it over the mortar, scooping a spoonful of the powder, and tapped it into the vial. Capping the vial, she shoved it back into the pocket, and repeated the process with the other nine bottles, rising only to exchange full vials for empty ones.

The day stretched on behind her. Her focus remained on the

mound of powder, which slowly decreased until the spoon scraped across the bottom of the stone bowl with every scoop. She shoved the stopper in the final bottle and stood, her muscles throbbing, stiff from her crouched position. She deposited the vials onto the bottom shelf but paused on the final vial, which felt unusually heavy.

"Zenna!"

She glanced toward the window. Mother never called her name, and only one other person knew she was here—Malik. Dropping the bottle into her apron, Zenna inched toward the window, her heart sputtering. She inhaled, placed her hand on the frame, then leaned out.

"What do you want?"

"I'd rather not yell it." Malik stared up at her from the base of the tower. "May I come up?"

"The stairs are broken."

If she were closer, she would have sworn he rolled his eyes.

"I'd like to try something."

"You already tried something." She arched an eyebrow.

"I didn't hear any complaints." Malik crossed his arms over his chest.

"That's because your fiancée wasn't here to witness your indiscretion."

"I am not engaged!" The snarl flew into the window and smacked her in the face, but she refused to step back from his anger.

"Your father says otherwise." She pulled the vial from her pocket, set it on the windowsill, and spun it. Violet sparkles flew over the frame.

"My father is a liar." Malik punched his fist into the side of the tower, then glanced over his shoulder. Lowering his voice, he hissed, "Dammit, Zenna, you're going to get me killed."

"Why does your father think you're engaged?" She slapped her hand on the bottle, stopping it mid-spin.

"If I promise to answer that question first, will you help me climb into the tower?" He lowered his voice and checked behind himself again.

"What do you mean climb?"

"I need you to trust me."

"I'm not certain I should." She tucked the vial back into her apron.

"I'm not either." He shifted, taking a third glance at the building in the center of the compound. "Wrap your hair around one of the armoire legs twice, then throw the rest out the window. Hurry, before someone discovers me out here, and we both receive punishment."

Zenna nodded and scampered from the window. Lifting the pile of coiled hair from the base of the staircase, she wrapped it around the armoire leg as instructed, then flung the rest out of the window.

"Good." He dug his fingers into the side of the tower and pulled himself up, scaling the side. "Next, grab onto your hair with both hands and brace your feet against the armoire."

She did as he directed and wound her hair around her arm for extra leverage.

"Okay."

"This is going to hurt." His voice floated over the windowsill.

"You're not selling me on this idea," she replied, tightening her grip.

She screamed out as Malik grabbed onto her hair. Each time he moved, his weight jerked her hair, the pain increasing with each pull. She sank her teeth into her lower lip to stifle her cries. Just his fingers appeared on the windowsill, she collapsed on the floor, agony coursing through her scalp.

He tumbled through the opening, twisted around mid-fall, and yanked her hair through the window in one smooth movement, pulling it from view. He dropped beside her, heaving.

"That seemed much easier in my mind," he said to the ceiling, his chest rising and falling in time with hers.

"How long did you consider it?"

"For most of the meeting." Rolling to his side, he reached out and laced his hand through hers.

"What did you do during the other portion?" she asked, distracted by the soft tickle of his thumb on her palm.

"Think about what I would do once I got up here." His eyes glowed.

"I believe you planned to give me a message." She pulled her hand from his and sat up. He sat up as well, adjusted a thin rope that crossed his chest, and leaned against the back of the sofa.

"Mother said he will be late picking up the batch. Something urgent has arisen." Malik waved his hand in a vague motion. "You have earned a reprieve."

"You could have told me that from the ground." Zenna frowned. Winding her hair around her arm, she mentally counted the loops. On the final wrap, she glanced up. "What of your engagement?"

"I am not engaged, and I have never been. My father wishes to attach me to one of the daughters of a rival boss to ease tensions between the two sides." Malik shifted and tugged at the strap again. "I have no intention of marrying Tessa or any other woman for the sake of his business."

"No one refuses your father." She shoved the bundle of hair underneath the armoire, unwrapping it from the leg.

"I did." He pulled the rope over his head and held out a small sack. "I brought you something."

"What is it?" Her gaze dropped to the bag.

"Take it."

She scuttled forward and snatched the sack from his outstretched hand. His other hand closed around her wrist and dragged her across the stone floor toward him.

"Let me go!" She swung the sack at his face, but he caught her other arm with his free hand and anchored them both behind her back.

"It's rude to hit someone who brings you a gift." His chastisement held a trace of humor. "Before you proceed with your misplaced vengeance, perhaps you should look in the bag."

"I can't, my arms are incapacitated." She glowered at him.

He snickered and released her. She sat back on her feet, smoothed the apron out over her legs, and placed the sack in her lap. After prying apart the strings, she stuck her hand in the bag.

"Grapes?" She pulled out a bunch of the deep purple fruit.

"Leftover from lunch." His mouth crooked into a sheepish grin. "There's cheese in there, too. I thought you might enjoy something other than bread and water."

Pulling off a grape, she placed it on her tongue and pressed the fruit against the roof of her mouth until it exploded, and juice rolled down her chin. She giggled and wiped her hand across her lips.

"Delicious."

"I brought you one other thing." He gestured to the bag. "Dig deeper."

Curious, Zenna stuck her hand back into the bag, and her fingers brushed over something cold and metallic. Shock vibrated through her body. She removed her hand from the sack and opened her palm—inside rested the silver heart necklace. Her head whipped up.

"Why would you do this?" she asked, her eyes widening. According to Mother, there was no greater offense than theft. Malik had condemned himself to death.

"It wasn't his to take." Leaning forward, Malik lifted the necklace from her hand and fastened it around her neck. His fingers lingered around her throat, drawing soft circles around the bruises left by Mother.

She grabbed Malik's hands, stilling them, and rose on her knees, leveling her gaze with him.

"Mother will kill you."

"Are you so concerned for my life? I thought you believed me a liar." He wiggled his eyebrows.

"You have redeemed yourself." Zenna released him. One fingertip stroked over the charm. "Thank you for returning the necklace, but I don't understand why you needed to climb up here to give it to me."

"My father commanded I return to my territory immediately, but I couldn't leave without..." He sighed and dragged a hand through his shaggy hair. "I've been with many women—I have quite a lot of experience in that particular pursuit—but I've never had the reaction I did when I kissed you this morning."

"You want to kiss me goodbye?" she asked, her voice laced with the confusion running wildly through her body.

"Goodbye, goodnight, good morning..." He inched closer, and his arms slipped around her neck.

"Dinner?"

Malik paused, his lips millimeters from hers. "Are you inviting me to dinner?"

"You did bring me grapes and cheese." She smiled.

"There's only one thing I want." His eyes blazing, he leaned forward and pressed his mouth to hers. Sliding his hands down her back, he grabbed her waist, yanking her on top of him. His hand moved down her hip, pushing aside the apron and slipping under the hem of her shirt, then closed around the knife strapped to her thigh.

"Armed again?" he murmured against her lips. Unfastening the strap buckle, he pulled the sheath from her leg and tossed it onto the sofa, his hand returning to her thigh.

She gasped as his tongue dove into her mouth, tangling with hers. His grip tightened, guiding her hips into a grinding motion as his hard length pressed between her thighs. Overwhelming sensations rolled through her limbs as if every nerve were alive and burning at the same moment. She feared her body would rip apart.

Breaking the kiss, Zenna tipped her head back, her body moving against Malik. Digging his fingers into her hips, he increased her tempo, his lips trailed across the hollow of her throat. Her stomach clenched, winding tighter and tighter.

"Malik." She panted his name, apprehension echoing in the room.

"Let go," he growled, the word vibrating through her body, and nipped at her throat.

"Ma—" She screamed, an explosion rocking her body. His arms wound around her waist pulled her roughly against his chest as she quivered. The tremors subsided, and she drew in a shaky breath.

"I assume that was a first," he said as she pushed away from him.

She nodded, acutely aware of the cool breeze blowing across her bare legs. Warmth spread through her face, the blush traveling through her skin until she was certain her entire body glowed pink.

Engines revved in the distance. Malik's head whipped toward the window, and he paled.

"Who is it?" Zenna whispered her question, knowing the answer before Malik spoke.

"He must have completed his business early." Malik turned his attention back to her, his eyes mirroring the fear bubbling in Zenna's chest. "Is there anywhere to hide?"

"The loft." She gestured at the staircase. "Mother never goes up there."

Malik nodded once and still holding Zenna, climbed to his feet. He drew one finger down the side of her cheek.

"I have a favor to ask of you."

"I won't say anything."

"That wasn't the favor." He set her down, then grabbing the

sack from the floor, and stuffed the grapes into the bottom. The sound of the motorcycles intensified, their thunderous roar echoed in the compound. He glanced up, an apology in his eyes.

"You need to give me the necklace."

She took a step backward and shook her head, her hand flying to the charm.

"You gave it to me."

"And I will give it back after my father leaves." His gaze flicked to the window. "We don't have much time."

Lifting her hand to the clasp, with trembling fingers, she unhooked the necklace and dropped it into the sack. Malik's eyes softening, he took her hand and raised it to his lips, brushing a gentle kiss across her knuckles.

"I'm not going anywhere. You owe me dinner, remember?"

She sank her teeth into her lower lip and nodded. The rumble of motorcycles vibrating through the tower, she gave Malik a shove toward the staircase. His heavy boots pounded on the steps as he sprinted toward the bedchamber.

Spinning around, she spied the tank top Malik had draped over the side of the sofa, grabbed the shirt, and wadded it into a ball just as Mother appeared beneath the staircase. She gasped and stumbled backward, bumping into the back of the sofa. Her gaze skipped up the stairs and stopped at the thin curtain covering the loft. It fluttered in the gentle afternoon breeze.

"What is that?" Mother stepped forward from the shadows, and his face contorted with rage.

Zenna glanced down at the shirt. "Blood."

"Whose is it?" Mother advanced, cracking his knuckles.

"M-M-Malik's."

"Why is it on your shirt?" His fingers closed around the cloth, and he jerked it from her fingers.

"You threw him against a wall."

"Did I?" Mother snickered, flinging the crumpled shirt at the sofa, where it landed on top of her knife. He walked to the window and stared out at the approaching evening. "Malik was to give you a message."

"He said you were delayed and would return later than expected to collect the vials." Zenna took one step toward him, placing her body between Mother and the staircase. "Then he left."

Mother spun around, his eyes dark. "I don't believe you."

4

Zenna swallowed, a bead of sweat slid down her back. "Why would I lie?"

"I don't know." Mother tilted his head. "But I have a theory, shall we test it?"

Without waiting for Zenna's response, Mother lunged forward and grabbed her by her shirt, his fingers crushing the thin material. Rotating his hand, he wound the shirt around his fist, lifted her from her feet, and flung her at the armoire. She smashed into the unforgiving wood and crashed to the floor, rolling in agony. A whimper crawled from her throat and floated toward the rafters, the only sound in the small chamber. The curtain fluttered.

Mother strode across the room and stopped at the base of the staircase, his hand gripping the banister. He turned and flashed an ominous smile at Zenna. Lifting one boot, he set it onto the first stair. The wooden step groaned under his weight. He hesitated, frozen halfway on the step.

"It wasn't built to support someone of your stature," she said, grimacing as she pushed up on trembling arms.

"You should know better than to insult me." He spun around, abandoning the staircase, and flowed toward her.

She curled away from his ire. "I was warning you."

Crouched beside her, his arm whipped out, and two thick fingers closed around her chin. Wrenching her head toward him, he dug his nails into her skin.

"I know you are hiding something from me." His deep growl sent a shiver down her spine.

Mother would drag the truth from her, and the punishment for hiding Malik would be far worse than being tossed at furniture. Her gaze flicked to the back of the tower, landing on the empty mortar, and immediately returned to Mother's scowl.

"You're right. There's something I need to tell you."

Mother arched an expectant eyebrow.

"I'm finished. That batch completes the final payment. My parents' debt is clear."

Mother threw her head down and stood. He walked to the shelves, his heavy footsteps echoed in the tower. His gaze slid across the vials. Selecting the nearest tray, he extracted one of the bottles.

"Do you know why my son was here today?" he asked, his back to Zenna.

"Because you asked him," she replied. A glint near the curtain caught her eyes. Malik peered around the edge, his face a mixture of fury and concern. She waved him back.

Mother snorted and uncorked the vial. He tilted back his head, swallowed the contents of the vial, and shuddered, then tossed the bottle into the mortar. It clinked against the sides as it settled in the bottom. Mother spun around, his eyes glowed black.

"I am expanding the distribution of Votras Alute. Soon, it will be available in every town along the coast." He grinned and snatched another bottle from the same rack.

"I don't understand." Zenna climbed to her feet, limped to the back of the sofa, and leaned against the shabby furnishing. "How will you produce it?"

"I have you." He lifted the second vial in salute to her and swallowed the contents. The tremor that rippled through his body took him to his knees, and sweat lined his forehead, dripping down the sides of his face.

"I have paid my debt." She wrapped her fingers around the back of the sofa and forced her voice to remain soft. Yelling at Mother only resulted in pain.

"Not by my calculation."

"I have recorded every bottle I created." Her chest squeezed the breath from her lungs. She felt as though she were drowning.

"I have no doubt." Mother approached her, dragging his feet along the floor. "However, you failed to take into account the money I have spent to keep you alive."

"You kidnapped me and held me captive." She took a step backward.

"I gave you a place to stay and food to eat while you worked off your parents' debt." He grabbed her wrist and yanked her body against his. One hand stroked her hair. "You owe me."

"How much?"

"Twenty years, shall we say ten thousand per year... two hundred thousand? Plus, whatever costs you incur while you are paying off that debt. It appears you'll be my guest for the next twenty years." He chuckled and combed his fingers through her hair. "And I have big plans for you."

Revulsion rolled through her stomach. Her fist clenched, vibrating beside her hip. If she struck Mother, he would beat her unconscious. And if Malik interfered...

"I want to see my parents," she replied, forcing her hand to relax one finger at a time.

"No." He released her and weaved toward the window, and his thighs bumped against the bottom of the sill. Lifting one leg, he stuck it out the opening, and sat, straddling the frame. Precariously balanced, he glanced over at her.

"Please." She took a step toward him, her hands clasped together. "I just want to tell them I'm alright."

"They won't remember you." He turned, wrapped his hands around the windowsill, and leaned out, his body nearly parallel with the ground.

"I am their daughter." Her fierce growl drew Mother's attention, and he twisted toward her, a strange glow lit his eyes. He gestured for Zenna to move closer. She took one hesitant step forward.

"What did Malik say before he jumped from the window?"

"That he hoped you were watching." She hovered just outside of his reach.

"Always looking for praise." Mother shook his head and pulled his other leg through the window, both his feet swinging freely over the courtyard. Crossing his arms over his chest, he dove forward.

Zenna screamed and dashed to the window. She peered down into the courtyard, searching for Mother's body. A soft moan drifted up from the ground, then laughter. It grew, the maniacal sound echoing in the tower.

"That's a pity." Malik's deep voice drew a shiver down her back. She spun around, finding him at the top of the staircase. "I had hoped he wouldn't survive the fall."

"Aren't you worried for him?" She waved her hand at the window. "He could die."

"Would that make your life worse?" He descended the staircase, pausing on the last step.

"You're not any nicer, remember?" Sinking onto the windowsill, she sighed. "What does it matter who I work for?"

He crossed the room and knelt at her feet, his head level with the bottom of the window. Peering over the edge, his gaze sought his father's crumpled form. Shouts echoed across the compound, followed by the thunderous echo of boots running toward Mother.

"I don't want you to work for me." Malik dropped back to the floor and pressed his back against the wall. Reaching up, he grabbed her arm and yanked her off the windowsill. She landed on top of him and shifted, straddling his legs. Slipping his arms around her waist, he pinned her to his lap. "I want you to date me."

"I'm certain you're not lacking for female companions."

"I'm not," he snorted. "But I've never met someone who didn't want anything from me. I find you intriguing."

"What happened?" A gruff voice laced with worry drifted into the tower.

"I jumped from the tower," Mother replied, pride saturated his statement.

"Why would you risk your life?"

"I was testing the potency of this latest batch of Votras Alute," Mother said.

"And?"

"We will be invincible, Jax." Mother's cackle of delight sent ice rippling through Zenna's veins. She shivered and pressed her face against Malik's chest.

"He's never going to let me go," Zenna said, her words muffled by Malik's shirt. "I'm going to die in this tower."

"Why didn't you tell Mother I was hiding upstairs?" Malik tipped her head, lifting her face until she stared into his eyes.

She bit her lip. "He would have killed you."

"He almost killed you."

"But he won't." She forced a smile, echoing Malik's earlier sentiment. "He needs me."

"Leave with me tonight. I can hide you in my city, my father will never find you. We'll cut your hair and escape. You won't have to make that horrible drug again."

"I can't." Zenna glanced down, the familiar feel of wetness building along her eyelashes.

I will not cry.

"You don't want to go with me?" The pad of his thumb brushed away one of the tears rolling down her cheek.

"Mother will kill my parents." She sniffed.

"I won't let him." Malik's arms circled her waist again.

"What can you do against a man as powerful as your father?" she whispered, fearing her voice would crack.

Malik's face darkened, fury poured from his body. She trembled, afraid of his anger, and shoved her hands between their bodies, wiggling in his iron embrace. The motion drew a groan from Malik. His arms constricted, pinning her to his chest.

"Stop struggling, or I will kiss you." His eyes blazed with blue fire.

"What did you say?" She froze, her fingers splayed across his chest.

"Hold still. I'm having a difficult time protecting your virtue at this moment." His lips brushed over her ear, sending tingles zipping through her veins. "And you're not helping."

"You said you wouldn't hurt me."

"Thus, your warning."

"I could sit beside you."

"You could, but I like your current position." Grinning, he leaned his forehead against hers. His lips lingered a millimeter away from hers, their tantalizing heat teasing her mouth.

"What if I wanted to kiss you?" Sliding her hands up his chest, Zenna wrapped her arms around his neck and pulled his head down.

Malik touched his mouth to hers, his tongue pushing past her lips. Her stomach clenched, tightening with expectation. Sliding his hands down her back, he grabbed her hips, jerking her against him, and guided her body into a rocking rhythm, the heat flaring between them.

"Can you do that thing to me again?" She panted against his mouth, her fingers digging through his hair.

"The thing that made you scream?" His hands cupped her butt, grinding his hips into her.

"Mmm," was all she could manage. Her head tipped back as the coil in her stomach wound tighter. She pushed herself against Malik, craving release.

"Malik!"

Their heads ripped apart, and Zenna found herself sitting on the cold stone floor. Malik, on his feet beside her, slowly lowered his fists and glanced down.

"It came from outside."

"What is the point of him having a mirror if he never answers my call?" Mother's rage-filled voice rose from the courtyard.

"A mirror?" Zenna asked, mouthing the words.

Malik dug into his pocket and extracted a small silver disk. He dropped beside her and held it out. It glowed.

"This is how we communicate. When I open it, the person on the other side can see and hear me."

"What happens if you don't open it?"

"It irritates my father."

She climbed to her knees and peered out the window. The last dregs of afternoon highlighted the back of Mother's head, glinting off his dark hair and giving him a surreal reddish glow. He stood without aid—a testament to the power of Votras Alute —in the center of the compound, surrounded by four men of similar surly attitude.

"Jax, find out if Malik made it back to his territory," Mother addressed the stout man to his right.

"Did he have an escort?" Jax asked.

"Why would he need one?" Mother scoffed. "He's my son."

"His saddlebags are loaded with Votras Alute." The other men in the group nodded their heads in concordance. "Several couriers have been attacked in the past few weeks. People are getting desperate."

"No one is foolish enough to touch Malik." Mother fiddled with the silver object in the palm of his hand, and the disc in Malik's hand glowed again.

"He's going to be really angry when he discovers you're in the tower." Zenna glanced at him.

"He won't." Malik thumbed at himself. "Knowing me, I probably stopped at a bar."

"And started a fight?"

Malik grinned. "That sounds like me."

The glow faded from Malik's closed mirror, and a flurry of curses followed.

"I want answers... now!" Mother's anger permeated the tower.

"I'll find him," Jax replied.

"Carlyle—"

"I don't need assistance." Jax's growl was met by silence. He rolled his shoulders forward, cowering in front of Mother's fury.

"Carlyle, I want you to guard the south tower." Mother turned, his gaze lifted to the window. Zenna ducked down. "No one enters, no one leaves. Jax will relieve you at midnight, where he will remain on duty if he returns without word of my son."

"Yes, Mother." Carlyle touched his hand to his forehead.

"Looks like I'm staying the night." Malik shoved the mirror into his pocket.

Zenna paled, her head whipping between him and the window.

Malik laughed. "I can sleep on the sofa."

"I wasn't thinking about that." Except now, she was thinking about it—the way his mouth moved over her skin, his body pressed hard against her. She blushed, heat crawling through her cheeks.

He arched an eyebrow, his lips twitched. "What were you thinking about?"

"Why would Mother assign a guard to my tower? He's never done that before."

"Ever?" Malik frowned.

"Do you think he suspects you're still here?"

"No one saw me climb up, I waited until they left." Malik shifted, digging his shoulder blades into the wall. "He must think you'll try to escape tonight."

"I wouldn't risk my parents' lives." Zenna drew a small circle on the floor.

"Yet Carlyle and Jax are spending the night beneath your window... You should introduce yourself."

"What purpose would that serve?"

"At some point, I'll need to leave. It would be easier if Carlyle were asleep when I climbed down."

"How would talking to him convince him to fall asleep?"

"You don't look threatening." Malik covered her hand with his. "He is kinder than Jax and will underestimate the situation."

She nodded and rose. Her gaze slid across the compound, searching for Mother. Neither he nor the other men were visible. Leaning out the window, she glanced down. Carlyle marched a lazy circle around the base.

"Hello," she said, cupping her hand around her mouth.

Carlyle ignored her.

"Hello!"

He flinched, then kept walking.

"I know you can hear me."

"So, what if I can?" He stopped and glared up at her.

"I have a question for you."

"I ain't helping you down."

"I wasn't going to ask you that."

"You don't want my help?" He pulled on the end of a long, salt-and-pepper beard and glanced over his shoulder as if he expected Mother to appear and castigate him for speaking to Zenna.

"Of course not." She gave him a winning smile.

"What do you want?" he asked, taking a step closer to the tower.

"Is Mother alright? He jumped from the window, and I wanted to confirm he was completely healed." Zella tilted her head.

"What does it matter to you?"

"I make the drug. I'd like to know the formula worked."

Carlyle choked. "You're the manufacturer?"

"What did you expect, a troll?"

"Well, no…" He tugged on his beard again. "Mother is fine, fully recovered."

"That is excellent. Thank you." She pulled her head back into the window. Her gaze dropped to Malik, and she shrugged. Malik held up his hand and counted down on his fingers. When he reached zero, Carlyle's voice echoed up from the ground.

"Miss?"

Malik grinned and gestured for her to answer.

"Yes?" she asked, leaning out again.

"Since I'm spending my evening guarding you, may I ask a favor?" Carlyle hovered underneath her window.

"There's not much I can do from up here."

"I've been having terrible aches in my leg, miss."

"He was shot several years ago during a hijack, saving my father's life," Malik murmured. His finger traced a light design over her bare foot. "The cold bothers his injury."

Zenna dipped her hand into the apron pocket and extracted the over-filled vial of Votras Alute. She held it out the window, allowing the setting sun to stream through the bottle.

"Mr…"

"Carlyle." His eyes followed the vial.

"Mr. Carlyle."

46

"Just Carlyle, miss."

"Carlyle, I do have one test bottle of powder from this morning's batch." She placed her hand on the windowsill and leaned further out, the vial clasped between two fingers. "However, I must warn you, this is a strong dose."

"I can handle it." His growl held a note of pride.

"What does that mean?" Malik muttered. Zenna's eyes flicked to him.

"It's a full vial, so this amount will cure his injury."

"Completely?" His eyes rounded. "Mother said that wasn't possible. He warned too much would cause a person to go insane."

"He lied."

"Carlyle was at my father's side when he took control from Bruno Rossi..." Malik's finger tapped a gentle rhythm on the top of her foot. "Give it to him."

She nodded and returned her attention to the man pacing back and forth in front of the tower.

"Ready?"

Carlyle stretched up his hand.

Zenna released the vial. Tumbling toward the ground, flipping end over end, painting deep purple sparkles across the tower, the bottle landed in Carlyle's gloved palm, and his fingers closed around the vial.

"Thank you, miss." He flashed her a smile, revealing a mouthful of chipped teeth, and slunk around the tower, hiding in the bushes which separated the tower from the main wall surrounding the compound.

"You've made a friend." Malik climbed from the floor.

"He won't cross Mother." Her eyes scanned the base of the tower as the final fingers of sunlight retracted from the grounds.

"You'd be surprised what people will do with the right motivation." Malik stepped behind her and wrapped one arm around

47

her waist. Brushing aside her hair, his mouth placed a searing kiss on the back of her neck. She shivered.

A whoop echoed across the compound. Carlyle burst out from behind the tower, running at full speed toward the center of the courtyard. He leapt over two stone benches, circled the courtyard once more, then vanished. In the darkness, a motorcycle roared.

"I wonder if he's coming back…" Malik chuckled, his lips tickled her skin.

Zenna stiffened. "You should leave."

"Are you throwing me out?"

"No." She spun around, her eyebrows pulled together. "But there is no longer a guard—"

Malik placed one finger over her mouth. "You invited me to dinner."

"What if Carlyle returns?"

"He owes you." Malik slid his arms around her waist. "As do I."

"What do you owe me?"

"I promised to make you scream again." He backed her against the wall. "And I rather enjoy hearing my name on your lips."

5

_____

Her stomach clenched, desire curled through her body, and a secondary emotion... fear.

"You seem very sure of yourself."

"I am." His fingers slid down her arm, and she trembled under his soft caress. He stepped back, a frown on his lips. "I don't think I've ever seen that reaction before."

"What reaction?"

"Terror." He stepped around her and crossed the room, heading for the staircase.

"I'm sorry." Her hands twisted together. "I..."

"Don't apologize." Malik paused at the base of the staircase and turned toward her, a peculiar expression on his face.

"But you're leaving."

"Am I?" He glanced up the staircase. "Is this the exit?"

"No..." She took a small step toward him. "I thought you were angry."

"Because you're frightened? I may look like my father, but I am not him." He abandoned the stairs, traversed the room in three strides, and gathered her in his embrace. "Zenna, I'm not going to force you to do something you're not ready to experience. I want you to be with me because you want to, not because of some misguided notion of repayment. Do you understand?"

She nodded once, sinking her teeth into her lip.

"I propose we eat dinner. You can tell me about your parents."

"My parents?" She blinked in confusion.

"Yes, any memory you have of them. What they looked like, where they lived, the last time you saw them." He released her and returned to the staircase. "If I'm going to find them, I need to know as much information as possible."

"I don't remember much," she said to his back, her soft reply barely carrying across the tower.

"What did you say?" He stopped at the top of the staircase and turned, his gaze seeking her.

She scooted into the center of the room, hovering on the opposite side of the sofa.

"I haven't seen or spoken to them since Mother took me."

"My investigation is based on the memory of a five-year-old." Malik shook his head, spun, and swiped the curtain aside, then leaned over and grabbed the sack from the center of the bed.

Sighing, Zenna turned away. She dragged to the sofa and collapsed. Only Mother knew the location of her parents, and he was never going to reveal that information. Hopelessness encompassed her. Drawing her legs into her chest, she slumped down, her forehead on her knees.

"I didn't say I couldn't do it." Malik's deep rumble startled her. Her head whipped up.

"How—"

"You have secrets; I do too." He dropped beside her and handed her the sack.

"I told you mine," she said.

"You did?"

"Kidnapped, maker of Votras Alute, never been kissed."

"You've been kissed."

Heat crept into her cheeks. "I meant before you."

"There better not be an after me." He wiggled his eyebrows, and she giggled. "Better. Now, let's start with an easy question. What are your parents' names?"

"My mother was called Anna." She closed her eyes, forcing her mind to filter through childhood memories long buried in her subconscious. The cushion beside her moved. Her eyes flew open, and she found Malik kneeling beside the fireplace.

"Continue." He waved his hand, his back to her.

"My father was Enzo... There's not enough woo—"

Malik moved aside. A blazing fire crackled, the heat from the fireplace coating her in a thick blanket of warmth.

"How did you do that?" she asked, setting the sack on the cushion beside her, and leaned forward.

"Votras Alute." He wiped his hands on his pants, leaving a smear of dark purple across his jeans. "Takes forever to burn too."

"How do you know that?" She approached the fireplace, hesitating, and knelt beside him. Holding her hands out, she rubbed them together.

"It's the only way to destroy the product; I've been hitting our couriers."

"You? Why?"

"Revenge. My father murdered my mother when I was fourteen."

The image of a boy kneeling on the ground in the courtyard exploded into her mind.

"Was that the day he whipped you?"

"He forbade me from speaking her name." Pain flashed through Malik's eyes. "I had hoped my father's supply of the flower would run out if I ruined enough of the drug. It was shocking to learn the flower is no longer the main ingredient."

"Is that why you want to help me escape, to punish your

father?" She edged away from him, moving as far as possible without leaving the heat of the fireplace.

"If I wanted to punish my father, I would have cut your hair and left you to his anger." Malik raised his hand, closing it around a golden strand, then dragged his fingers down the tress and tucked it behind her ear. "Yes, there is the added benefit of revenge if you come with me. However, if I can't locate your parents and must climb up here every day to see you, so be it."

"You're going to climb up here every day just to see me?"

"I'd prefer to do other things to you too, but…"

"Show me." She was not given to rash decisions, but the reality of eternity weighed on her mind. Tonight could be her last moment of human contact, save her exchanges with Mother.

"Zenna." Hesitancy saturated the word.

She scowled, pushed off the floor, and stalked to the window. Leaning out, she grabbed one shutter and pulled it closed, then repeated the process with the other shutter and latched the two of them together. When she finished, she spun around.

"I don't know the depth of your talents, but there is a high probability you will not find my parents, or worse, Mother will discover your plan. If I'm going to be trapped in this tower for the rest of my life…"

"You're not."

"You can't know that!" She untied the half-apron, ripped it from her waist, and slammed it down on the sofa, her heart hammering. "Your father controls what I wear, what I eat, where I sleep, and until now, who I see. You are my only chance to defy him."

Malik opened his mouth.

She held up her hand. "Please, don't tell me no."

"Why would I tell you no?" He climbed to his feet and dragged a hand through his hair. "You should know, you look absolutely petrified."

"I am."

"That's not really a motivating factor in my decision."

"Do you want me to beg?"

A whisper of a smile crossed his mouth. "I do, but not yet."

"Does that mean yes?"

"Are you certain you want to do this?"

"Absolutely." Her head bobbed, a violent answer to his question.

He closed the distance between them and wrapped his arms around her waist.

"Promise me, you'll tell me the moment you change your mind."

"I'm not going to."

"How did you get to be so stubborn?" He cupped her face, his thumb skated across her lower lip.

"Years of practice." She shivered, her eyes half-closed.

"Something my father never managed to beat from you?" he whispered.

"He didn't beat it from you either."

"True."

Before she could react, Malik scooped her into his arms.

"What are you doing?" She squealed in shock.

"Taking you upstairs." He leaned his forehead against hers. "I'd prefer a bed to the sofa, and yours is very comfortable."

"It can't be finer than yours."

"It's not," he grinned. "But mine doesn't have you in it."

He snagged the quilt and the small sack from the sofa, crossed the room in three steps, and dashed up the staircase. After spreading out the quilt, he set her in the center of the bed, dropped the sack on the floorboards, and spun around. Dragging her hair up the steps, he wound it around his arm and piled the golden mass on the floor at the foot of the bed.

"Before I'm distracted, is there anything else you remember

about your parents like their last name?" he asked, glancing over at her.

"No." She chewed on her lip. Should she tell him? It was a nagging suspicion, one that had bothered her for years. "My name isn't Zenna."

Malik frowned. "What is it?"

"I don't know, but I feel in my heart that Zenna is wrong. My name began with an 'R'"

"My father is an intelligent man. Changing your name would help hide you, especially if your parents were looking for you." Malik pulled the curtain across the opening, plunging them into semi-darkness. The light from the fireplace danced across the ceiling, painting exotic shapes over the loft. "What about sounds or smells?"

Zenna squeezed her eyes shut. "Water. I could hear water through my bedroom window."

"Rushing water or crashing waves?"

"I don't know the difference."

"Don't be ashamed." His hand covered hers, and her eyes flew open. "I can work with what you gave me. It may take a while, but it's not hopeless."

Removing his shirt, he tossed it toward the end of the bed. The flickering firelight emphasized the muscles on his broad chest and danced over his muscular arms, highlighting a thick black band of thorns tattooed around his bicep. Zenna's reply stuck in her throat. Reaching out, she touched one tentative finger to a faint line carving its way across his abdomen. He sucked in a sharp breath as her fingernail scratched along the scar.

"What happened?"

"I don't always make the best choices." Malik gave her a wry grin. "I deserved that one."

"And the person who did this to you?"

"He's no longer alive."

She gulped, her eyes widening.

"I make no apologies for what I've done. My past is part of who I am," he said.

"But Votras Alute doesn't leave scars. Why do you have one?"

"I didn't use it," he replied, a slight note of pride in his statement. "I refused treatment."

"You could have died." She traced the scar.

"I wanted to… I deserve to…" He grabbed her hand, stilling her fingers. "I am not a good man."

"I've heard about your reputation."

"What do you know?" She shrank away from his growl, but his grip tightened, pinning her hand flat against his chest.

"When the wind blows in from the north, the breeze brings the men's voices into the tower." She gestured toward the curtain. "I usually can block them out… but sometimes, I listen."

"What do they say about me?"

"That you are unbending,"—Malik's mouth twitched as if he were pleased by the description—"and you have a lot of women."

"That's all?"

Snatches of conversations swirled in her mind, stories of torture and death. Malik's cruelty was well-known—and often spoke of—by Mother's crew, some in awe, others in terror.

"You are an exact replica of your father, cruel and compassionless." Underneath her hand, his heart thudded a rapid rhythm. She placed her other hand on top of his. "But you also offered to rescue a damsel in distress."

"My motives aren't pure."

"Are you trying to talk me out of this?"

"Yes."

"No one is forcing you." Pulling her hand free, she drew back against the post.

"Damn it, Zenna!" He slammed his hand on the bed. She jumped. "I defied my father, stole a necklace, and climbed a tower. The question is not if I'm attracted to you."

"Then—"

He crushed his mouth to hers. Dragging her toward him, he lifted her from the bed and pulled her onto his lap, her knees straddling his legs. His tongue plunged past her lips, accompanied by a growl which rumbled deep in his throat. Her head swam, dizzy from his sensuous assault. Clinging to his shoulders, her fingers dug into the hard muscle.

Sliding up her arms, his fingers drew a blazing path of desire, every inch of skin burning beneath his touch. His hands closed around the tank top straps and tugged the material down, revealing her breasts. She froze, heat crawling through her face. Malik pulled back, his eyes searched hers.

"I've never been undressed by anyone." She lowered her gaze as she murmured the admission. He hooked his fingers under her chin, lifting her face.

"It is my pleasure to volunteer."

She offered him a small smile, the best she could manage through the apprehension plaguing her mind. A decision, her decision—one Mother had no control over—yet an overwhelming sense of foreboding washed through her as if more rested upon this choice than she understood.

"You are overthinking this." Malik set her beside him, then pulled off his boots, dropping them on the floor, one heavy thud at a time. Rising, he spun around, facing her, and indicated his pants. "Take them off."

She nodded, her lower lip trapped between her teeth, and moved to the edge of the mattress. Her hands reached out, closed around his belt, and trembling fingers yanked the belt free of its buckle. Glancing up at him, he remained motionless, a stoic expression on his face. After a deep breath, she unbuttoned his pants, and they fell from his hips and pooled around his feet, revealing his hard length, which strained against black boxer-briefs.

Pushing off the bed, she stood, their bodies almost touching, and placed one trembling hand on his stomach, just above the band of his underwear. Malik's eyes glowed.

She gasped when he dragged the back of his knuckle across the exposed swell of her breast. He rolled her shirt down her torso, tugged it over her hips, and it fell to the floor. Even with the additional warmth of the fire, a shiver rolled down her back. She crossed her arms in front of her body, covering as much of herself as possible.

"You are beautiful." Malik grabbed her wrists and peeled her hands away from her skin, walking her backward until her legs bumped into the mattress. "Last chance to change your mind."

She shook her head, unable to trust her voice. Guiding her down onto the bed, he scooted to the side, so only half his body covered hers, and his erection dug into her thigh. One fingertip drew a lazy circle across her breast, circling her nipple. She wiggled, the sensation sending bolts of lightning ricocheting through her veins. His mouth claimed hers, his tongue plunged past her lips and drew a moan from her.

Sliding down her body, his hand reached the apex of her thighs, then dipped between her legs. She cried out, arching her back as one digit plunged into her core. Malik's finger retracted, caressing her nub gently, then dove back into her center again, his finger matching the rhythm of his tongue.

She panted under his ministrations, her stomach winding tighter, and her fingernails raked along the bed. Malik's finger increased its tempo—stroke, thrust, repeat—until she could do nothing but writhe on the bed, her hips lifting to meet his hand with desperate urgency.

Her release came suddenly, crashing over her in waves of unyielding tremors, her passion-filled voice echoing in the chamber. When the tingling sensations subsided, she drew in a shaky breath, and her gaze slid to Malik.

"I'm going to do the same thing to you again," he said, shedding his boxer-briefs. "Except this time, I'm not going to use my hand."

She nodded, a small tendril of fear growing in her mind.

Malik pushed her legs apart and rolled on top of her, settling between her thighs. His fingers skimmed down her torso, tickled her stomach, then slipped between them and brushed over her center. Angling his body, he thrust forward, burying himself in one quick stroke, and she cried out. He paused, melded with her, his eyes on her face.

"I'm sorry." Concern rumbled through his voice. "I've been told it can hurt the first time."

She chewed her lip and shifted beneath him. The sharp pain had faded, and she was left with a peculiar feeling of fullness.

"Does it hurt the second time too?"

"No." He chuckled and brushed a kiss over the tip of her nose. "Nor any time after that."

"Are you certain?"

"Fairly, but you can let me know."

Malik's hand teased her nipple, rolling the bud between his thumb and finger. She gasped, and her stomach clenched.

"You're making it difficult to concentrate."

"Good," he replied.

He lowered his head, and his tongue swirled around her breast, his teeth nipping at her sensitive skin. His hips began a slow rhythm, retracting and driving forward, each deliberate thrust accompanied by the silky caress of his lips. Moving across her collarbone, lingering on her throat, he kissed her fevered skin. Her lips parted when his mouth found hers. As he drove into her, his tongue slid into her mouth.

She wrapped her arms around him, her fingers digging into his back, and lifted her pelvis as he plunged forward, grinding her hips against him. He groaned, his rhythmic thrusting increasing in tempo. The coil of passion winding in her stomach tensed. She arched her back, pressing her body into him, her breath coming in short gasps. She needed the release, craved it like she craved his mouth on her skin.

"I want to hear my name on your lips," he ground out, his voice straining, and slammed into her. The unforgiving pace of his thrusts ignited her blood and sent fire racing through her limbs, burning every nerve until she thought her skin would melt from her bones.

"Malik!"

She screamed, her voice ricocheted off the walls, as the orgasm ripped through her and clung to him, violently shaking. He drove into her, relentlessly thrusting, his hands crushing the pillow beneath her head as he plunged deeper. He yelled out, his guttural cry overtaking hers, and collapsed on top of her, their harsh breathing the only sound in the room.

"I would very much like to do that again," Malik said after a minute. He crawled off her, drew her trembling body against his chest, and his mouth brushed over her forehead.

"But you need to leave before your father discovers you up here." She shivered as his fingertip skated over her hip.

He nuzzled her neck. "I think death might be worth spending the night."

"Would you rather have one night or the rest of your life?" She panted, angling her head to the side and exposing her throat to his lips.

"Are you proposing to me?" He drew back with mock indignation, his hand flew to his chest. "I'll never live down the shame."

"No." Horror spread through her. "I didn't mean…"

"I'm teasing." Malik laughed, the warm sound blanketed her. "Nothing can be done regarding that particular subject until I find your parents."

He gave her a quick kiss, sat up, then climbed from the bed. She pulled the thin sheet over herself as he gathered his clothing from the floor. After yanking on his boxer-briefs and pants, he dug into his pocket and extracted the silver disc. Dropping beside her on the bed, he held out his hand.

"You can use this to communicate with me. Until I come back for you, you must pretend everything is normal. Don't give my father any reason to suspect there is something amiss. Make the drug, pay your debt."

She glanced at his hand. "What if you don't come back?"

"I will return for you." His forceful growl caused her to jump. She accepted the mirror and held it up, the dull silver glinting in the dim glow of the firelight.

"If Mother discovers you are helping me escape, he will kill you, son or no." Her finger traced the outside of the mirror. "Why are you doing this?"

"I like you, and I take care of the things I like."

"I am not a thing." Sitting up, the sheet fell, gathering around her waist. His eyes flicked over her skin, then rose, glowing with hunger.

"You are a temptress." He reached out, his hand halfway to her breast, then paused and shook his head, lowering his arm. "What I want to do to you should not be rushed, and by the time I have finished, you'll have lost your voice."

Heat exploded in her face, crawling down her neck. Yanking the sheet over her chest, she tucked it under her arms.

"I am concerned about leaving you to my father. He'll be livid about Carlyle's disappearance and looking for someone to punish." Malik dragged a hand through his hair, worry etched deep lines in his forehead. "I won't be able to protect you..."

"I've survived twenty years without you," she replied and leaned forward, feeling along the floorboards for her long shirt.

Malik snatched the shirt away from her hand and, dangling it from two fingers, held it out, a daring smirk on his lips. She grabbed for it, but he caught her arm and hauled her body against his, pulling her onto his lap. Straddling him, her breasts crushed against his chest. His mouth brushed over hers, teasing.

"Carlyle?" Jax's voice drifted up from the ground. "Where are you? Carlyle!"

Zenna and Malik froze, their arms entwined.

Jax cursed.

"Mother, we have a problem."

6

———————

Malik hissed and quietly set her on the bed. Bending over, he yanked his boots onto his feet and leaned to his left to retrieve his shirt from the floor. He whipped it over his head and turned to her. Pressing his mouth to hers, he kissed her, his rough assault bruising her lips, and broke away.

"Sunset, three days. Use the mirror to contact me."

Rising, he pulled the curtain aside and peered out. He slipped past the flimsy material and headed down the staircase, balancing on his toes, so his heavy boots didn't echo in the tower. Zenna dragged her shirt up her legs, shoved her arms through the straps, and padded to the top of the staircase.

Taking two vials of Votras Alute, Malik uncorked them and swallowed the contents of both, his back to Zenna. Convulsions jerking his body, he groaned and stumbled, catching his balance on the small worktable. Discarding the bottles in the mortar beside his father's empty vials, he turned and lumbered toward the window.

Pressing his head against the shutter, he listened. After a moment, he unlatched the shutter and pushed it partially outward. Climbing into the open space, he glanced back at

Zenna and winked, then stepped from the window and vanished.

She screamed, clamping her hand over her mouth immediately, and raced down the staircase. Leaning out the window, she searched the darkness for Malik. Minutes crawled by. A shadow slunk beneath the window, and Malik's shaggy head appeared. He raised his arm in a salute and crept across the courtyard, disappearing just as Mother exploded from the building in the center of the compound.

"How can Carlyle be missing?" Mother's anger whipped across the compound.

"I don't know," Jax replied. "When I returned, he wasn't at his post."

Mother swung, his fist striking Jax in the stomach. Jax crumbled to the ground, a soft moan accompanying his fall. Mother stepped over his limp body and strode across the compound, heading for Zenna's tower.

She squeaked, grabbed the shutter, and yanked it closed. After latching the wood, she backed away, turned, and darted up the staircase. Diving behind the curtain, she jerked it across the opening to her loft, and her gaze slid over the small enclosure. She snatched up the mirror and the small sack, leapt onto the bed, and shoved them both under her pillow. Ripping the covers over her head, she waited, her heart thudding, hammering a loud rhythm of terror. Had Mother seen her?

No sound came from outside the tower. Shoving off the sheet, she climbed from the bed, crept to the curtain, and pulled it aside. Mother's angry face waited on the opposite side. Screaming, she stumbled backward and crashed into the bed.

"Where is he?" Mother growled and stepped forward, his face hidden in shadow.

"Who?"

Mother's hand whipped out and closed around her neck, pinning her against the bedpost.

"Carlyle, the man I assigned to guard your tower."

Zenna's fingernails dug into his hand, prying his iron grip loose, tears streamed down her face. She gulped in a deep breath.

"He left."

"Did he say why?"

She shook her head, her eyes darting left and right. There was nowhere to go.

"What did you do?"

"I gave him a full dose of Votras Alute." The words burst out of her mouth. Mother's hand flew, smacking her across the face, and the taste of copper filled her mouth.

"Why would you do something so stupid? You could have killed him."

"You know it won't."

Her quiet statement enraged Mother. His hand sailed in the opposite direction, slapping her other cheek, and stars exploded behind her eyes. A barrage of blows followed, each one rattling her teeth as they landed. He released her, and she slumped to the floor, a puddle of agony.

Mother knelt beside her, pulled out a handkerchief, and wiped his hand on the cloth, taking care to remove the blood from his cuticles.

"I'm adding the cost of Carlyle to your debt. Shall we say, another ten years?"

"He was in pain," she replied and cried out as anguish radiated through her jaw.

"And now you're in pain." He leaned forward, resting his hand on his leg. "Was it worth it, helping another individual?"

"Yes." She glared at him.

Flinging the handkerchief at her face, he straightened. His gaze slid over the small space.

"Did Malik have anything to do with your sudden compassion for his Uncle Carlyle?"

Uncle? Why had Malik not mentioned that connection?

"Compassion is not a word I'd associate with your son." She pressed the handkerchief to her mouth. "Or with you."

"And you think you know my son's nature?" His eyes dropped to her.

"He was raised by you." Using the mattress for support, she climbed from the floor and leaned against the bedpost. Swiping her hair from her face, she winced as her fingers passed over a bruise blossoming on her cheek.

Mother nodded, seemingly satisfied with her response, and turned toward the staircase. The floorboards creaked as he clomped toward the landing. He froze as if debating the weakness of the wood, waved his hand, and vanished. Reappearing beside the shelves of Votras Alute, his mouth pressed into a hard line.

"There are bottles missing." He glared up at her, holding four empty vials in his hand.

"Two of them were yours, the other two, I used," she replied, hesitant to leave the loft. Malik's scent permeated the small space, wrapping around her in a comforting embrace.

"You used them?" Mother snarled, flinging the vials at the fireplace. They exploded, spitting shards of glass across the floor. He stomped to the center of the tower. "Come here."

She swallowed. Rolling her shoulders back, she exited the loft and walked down the staircase, her legs threatening to buckle. She crossed the floor and stopped just outside Mother's reach.

"Closer," he said, his voice sent a shiver of terror rippling through her body.

She took one more step.

Mother's heavy hand landed on her shoulder and pinched her flesh, threatening to crack her bones between his thick fingers. He jerked her to him, his mouth moved over her ear in an intimate caress.

"You stole from me."

She swallowed the disgusted lump in her throat and forced

65

her voice to remain even.

"I needed them to deconstruct the last batch."

"Since when?"

"You said this was one of my better ones." She cringed under his grip. "I wanted to recreate it."

"Why?" His eyes glowed black.

"A better product means less of the drug is needed per vial. It would increase my output and pay off the debt faster... especially now that you have added Carlyle's worth to my obligation."

Mother threw back his head and laughed, the horrific sound reverberating through the tower, growing to a deafening cackle.

"Ingenious!" He released her and spun toward the shelves. She staggered away from him and slipped around the sofa. Rubbing at her ear, her skin crawled.

Clapping his hands together, he lifted one arm, slashed it in a figure eight, and the vials disappeared. He repeated the gesture a second time, and empty, pristine vials reappeared in the racks. Jerking his head toward the sofa, he indicated a large burlap sack that rested on the cushions.

"I brought you a few things, water, food, clothing." His gaze slid down her shirt, stopping at her exposed thigh, a sinister gleam flashing in his eyes. "Your outfit is quite inappropriate. Were I a different man..." His voice trailed off, leaving his disturbing sentence unfinished.

"Thank you," Zenna said, not because she was grateful, but because he expected her appreciation.

"Warm in here this evening." He glanced at the fireplace, a pensive expression on his face.

Zenna gulped. If he figured out the fire was fueled by Votras Alute, his fury would be unparalleled. She took a step toward the fireplace.

"It's not any different from any other night." At least, it wouldn't be anymore, now that she knew she could use the drug for warmth. "You rarely visit me this late."

Mother strolled across the tower and stopped beside her. His gaze flicked to the locked shutters.

"If you give any more of that drug to my men, I will kill the recipient—and his family—in front of you. Sympathy has no place in my business. Do we understand each other?"

"Yes, Mother," she replied and cast her eyes down.

He evaporated without another word.

When she heard his barked command below the window, she exhaled a shaky breath and wobbled to the sofa. After collapsing on a cushion, she dragged the sack onto her lap and pried open the strings.

A loaf of bread, a leather canteen of water, and... another of Malik's old shirts. Holding the material up to her chest, she frowned. Was Mother kidding? Why would he condemn her outfit, then give her the exact same thing to wear? She held it to her face and inhaled, hoping the shirt held Malik's intoxicating scent. It didn't. Dejected, she balled it up and tossed it at the far side of the sofa, where it landed on top of her sheath and hid the knife's silver handle.

Three days.

The bruising on her face would vanish before then, and Malik would never learn the extent of the injuries his father inflicted upon her this evening. She was certain his reaction would be irrational and violent. Wincing, she rubbed her jaw. It felt broken. Her gaze flicked over the empty vials lining the wall. Even if she had a full bottle, she wouldn't touch it. Votras Alute did nothing to ease her pain.

This was not the first time Mother had fractured her bones. He nearly beat her to death at the age of ten. A batch, mixed with an incorrect amount of ginger root, paralyzed his face for five minutes. Once the drug wore off, he retaliated, pummeling her tiny body with his fists, then ripping a chunk of hair from her head. He left her on the floor of the tower, unconscious, surrounded by smashed vials—bits of glass embedded in her scalp—and covered in lavender powder.

She woke alone, her throat raw from crying. The tower, dark and cold, offered no comfort. Not one sound came from outside, no chirping birds, no revving motorcycles, and no rumbling whispers. The compound was deserted. She dragged her bloody body through the broken glass and collapsed beside the sofa where she lay motionless for hours, the only indication of time passing the movement of the shadows across the tower. The next morning, she gathered enough strength to pull herself onto the sofa.

Two days later, Mother reappeared. He bent over her body, his face emotionless.

"I am surprised to find you alive. You must be stronger than I expected, or perhaps I wasn't harsh enough on you."

She rolled away from him, facing the back of the sofa.

"I tried to recreate the drug yesterday." Mother shoved her legs aside and sank down on a cushion, resting his large hand on her foot. "Except the hair I took from you had turned grey. The test vial I gave to Bear took years from his life. He's an old man now."

Mother paused, and the hand resting on Zenna's foot flexed, one finger stroking along her instep. She longed to yank her leg away from him but feared the repercussions of that decision. Instead, she said nothing, refusing to flip over.

"Did you know that would happen?" His hand tightened, compressing the bones in her foot.

She cried out, twisting toward him. "No!"

Releasing her foot, he collected a small section of her hair from the floor, then reached into his boot, yanking out a small knife. Flicking his wrist, he extended the knife blade and sliced it across the piece of hair. He sat stoically and watched the golden color drain from the strand. Ten minutes. His menacing gaze rose from the grey tress.

"I'm sorry I made the batch wrong," she blurted out, her small voice shook with terror. "I will never do it again."

Mother nodded and discarded the grey hair on the floor.

"That batch does not count toward your parents' debt. Faulty product will not be rewarded."

"Will Bear be alright?" she asked, swallowing a groan as she moved onto her back.

"Probably not. You will lose several months of production while you are healing. He won't survive that long."

"I can start tomorrow." She sat up, hooking her arm over the back of the sofa, and leveled her gaze.

"I admire your spirit, but I have men who can't return for weeks after receiving a beating like the one you deserved." He tilted his head, his gaze sliding over her face. "Yet, you seem remarkably improved... What did you do?"

"I don't know... sleep." She shrugged, her confusion evident.

"You didn't take any of the drug?" Mother's dark eyebrows shot up.

She shook her head. "It's odd to swallow something made from my hair."

Leaning forward, Mother grabbed her wrist and drew it toward him. His other hand, still clutching the knife, slashed across her palm. She shrieked and jerked her arm as blood appeared along the gash. Mother's fingers tightened, cutting off the circulation to her hand. Slowly the wound closed itself, the puckered scar fading from bright pink to white and vanished completely.

"Incredible," Mother said. "It must be a side effect of the plant your mother ingested during pregnancy."

His eyes glowed black as he sliced the knife across her hand again and again. Blood flowed down her arms in rivulets. She spent another six days confined to the sofa, her incapacitation the direct result of Mother's perverse curiosity.

Bear did not die, but Mother's gratitude was short-lived, and he resorted to weekly punishments as motivation, pushing her body to the brink with torture before leaving her shattered on the floor. She spent four months in agony, unable to recognize her face in the mirror, which hung over the fireplace. Then, Malik arrived, and Mother turned his demonic attention to grooming his son.

What horrific nightmare had Malik suffered at the hands of his father? The image of a young Malik kneeling before his father's whip flashed into her mind. She glanced toward the window, overcome with sorrow. Mother had destroyed so many lives. A light breeze pushed the shutters inward, allowing moonlight to stream through the crack and blinding her momentarily. Was the same moon shining down on Malik?

Three days seemed an eternity to wait, and she could only think of one way to distract her fevered mind from endless worry—make more powder. She rose from the sofa, collected the loaf and canteen, and shoved them into the burlap sack. She hung the sack from the hook beside the shelves, returned to the sofa, and grabbed her apron. Tying the apron around her waist, her eyes skimmed across the sofa, searching for the knife. She retrieved it and the sheath from beneath Malik's old shirt.

Limping to the wall behind her worktable, she fastened the sheath to her leg, then pulled several jars of ingredients from the back wall, including ginger root and ground thistle. She set the jars beside the mortar, her gaze drifting up to the loft. Shaking her head, she forced her attention back to the jars. Using the metal spoon, she scooped out the ingredients, measuring them with precision. After returning the jars, she sank onto the stool and hooked her feet around the base of the table. She picked up the pestle and began the laborious process of grinding the herbs into a fine dust.

A prickly feeling crawled through the back of her neck. She set down the pestle, stretched her aching muscles, and glanced up at the loft. Malik had said three days... but what if he completed the task early and was trying to contact her? Was there any harm in checking the mirror? A small bubble of hope hovered in her chest.

She dashed up the staircase and jumped onto the bed. Rooting under the pillow, she extracted the mirror. It glowed brightly. Malik! She was going to be free! Prying the compact open, she held up the mirror, elation gushing through her veins.

Mother stared back, his mouth twisted into a dark grin. "Zenna? This is a delightful surprise. I knew Malik was plotting something, but I had no idea he was so taken with you."

"Where is he?" Zenna asked. She clutched the mirror, its edges leaving deep ridges in her hand.

"He's receiving punishment for treason."

"He's done nothing wrong."

Mother arched an eyebrow. "He's been meddling with my production."

"I've already started the next batch. There's been no inter-ference."

"How quickly you defend him." Mother smirked as Malik's strangled cry erupted behind him. "What has led to your sudden loyalty? Has Malik been feeding you false promises?"

Zenna swallowed, struggling to keep her face neutral. "He has not."

"Yet here you are, at the other end of the mirror." Mother tilted his head. "How did you come by this magical artifact?"

"I found it on the floor of the tower. It was glowing, so I picked it up and opened it." She offered him an innocent smile. "It could have fallen from Malik's pocket when you threw him against the wall."

"It could have… however, Malik already admitted he gave it to you." An anguished howl followed Mother's statement.

The mirror went dark.

7

"**M**alik!" Zenna screamed, shaking the mirror. She snapped it shut, smashed it against her palm, and wrenched the mirror open again. "Please answer."

Fog swirled in the looking glass. She sank onto the floor, a sob caught in her throat. Malik had risked his life to rescue her, now he was dead or would be by sunrise, and it was all her fault. She should have refused Malik, forced him to leave her tower.

"Siren!" The snarled word swirled up the staircase, laced with hatred. "You've twisted my son into a traitor."

A sharp pain exploded in her head. Her head jerked sideways, and the mirror slipped from her fingers and disappeared beneath the bed. Her body was dragged out of the loft. She rolled to her side, her fingers grabbing for the curtain. The curtain swung away, blown by a phantom breeze. Splinters dug into her back as she was yanked across the landing. She twisted, her tear-filled gaze landed on a dark figure.

At the foot of the staircase, Mother vibrated, a menacing scowl stretching his lips into a horrific glower. Around his arm, wrapped like a golden sleeve, was her hair. Reaching up with his free hand, he grabbed a section of tautly stretched hair.

Zenna cried out as he dragged her down the staircase, her body smashing on each step. Falling to the bottom of the staircase, she landed at Mother's feet, a pool of pain and limbs. He flung her hair on top of her, covering her face with the heavy mass. Before she could move, his steel-tipped boot sank into her ribs with a sickening crack. She shrieked, writhing in agony. He kicked her again, striking the same side, and Zenna's suffering echoed in the tower.

"By the time I'm finished, you'll have lost your voice," Mother mocked Malik's earlier sentiment.

"Were you listening to us?" Horror drowned out her anguish.

He bent over, leaning on one knee, and wound his fingers through her hair, his fingers scratching over her scalp and tightening. He jerked her head from the floor and brushed his lips over her ear. Revulsion churned through her veins.

"Mother is always listening." His voice pulsed with a whisper of something malevolent.

"What did you do to Malik?" she asked, pushing up on her arms, biting back a whimper.

"I punished him." Mother straightened, his iron grip lifting her from the floor.

Her hands flew up and grabbed his wrist, her fingernails carving deep gouges in his skin. With her hair wrapped around his fist, he dragged her through the tower, her heels scraped along the cold stone floor, leaving a crimson trail of blood from the base of the staircase to the rear of the tower. He discarded her beside the worktable.

"He was your son," she said, wheezing, and curled around the base of the table.

How much had Malik suffered? A small part of her hoped his death had been quick, even though Mother was not given to displays of compassion. She feared Mother's discovery of Malik's interference and his involvement in the destruction of product, had resulted in a torture session to rival any previous exchange she had witnessed.

Wordlessly, Mother yanked her from beneath the table and threw her at the wall. She smashed into the fireplace, just below the mirror, and fell to the floor. Mother advanced, his heavy boots echoing like thunder. She scrambled to her knees, hissing as a sharp pain flashed in her ribs, and her arms gave out. Collapsing, her chin hit the stone floor with a sickening thud.

A short bark of laughter ripped over her head as Mother clumped around the side of the sofa, the tips of his boots pausing at the top of her head. He pressed his shoe into her temple and rolled her face sideways, forcing her to stare up.

"Are you going to beg me to stop?"

"I will never beg you." She glared at him, tears streaming down her face. "You can't kill me, you need me to produce your filthy drug."

Mother removed his boot and crouched, balancing on the balls of his feet. He pinched Zenna's chin, lifting her head from the floor again.

"You're correct." A sinister gleam flashed in his eyes. "But I can hurt you really bad."

"If I'm in pain, I won't be able to make Votras Alute." Her lip trembled. Mother did not understand the word 'mercy.'

"You will make it, or I will extend your punishment to your parents." He rose and paced toward the shuttered window, stroking his chin. Snapping his fingers, he spun around, his eyes alight. "How about I give your mother to my men, and they can work out their frustrations on her body? I'm not certain she'll withstand the attack, but if she survives, you can nurse her back to health with the drug you'll be forced to create. Your father's punishment will be to witness your mother's suffering and to know you could have saved her from that horrific fate but failed."

"I hate you," Zenna's growl rumbled around the room.

Mother crossed the tower, hooked his hand around her hair,

and yanked her torso up, bending her backward into an unnatural position. Zenna cried out, her screams rising in volume as Mother torqued her body.

"You took my son from me." He flung her away.

"He wanted to be free," Zenna replied, her voice dripped with agony.

Dropping to the floor, Mother straddled her legs, pinning her with his bulk. The stones dug into her hips, slicing up the exposed skin of her thighs. His hands slid up to her shoulders, then constricted, crushing her bones.

"I would have made him a king." He leaned forward, his pelvis pressed into the small of her back. His mouth returned to her ear. "Why don't you do to me what you did to my son... maybe I'll let you go?"

"No!" She wriggled underneath him but could not throw him off her. With a screech, she whipped her head back, striking Mother in the face.

He howled and released her, jumping to his feet. She flipped over and scrambled away, scuttling backward until the sharp edge of the worktable stabbed her spine. Blood gushed from Mother's nose, streaming down his chin, and dripped onto his boots. He wiped his hand across his face, smearing the bright crimson over his chin. He glanced down at his hand, then lifted his malicious gaze to her.

"If I had known you would be this much trouble, I would have taken your mother instead and filled this tower with my children."

Zenna gasped. Delight flitted across Mother's face.

"You didn't know?" He stepped forward, his lip curled into a snarl. "Your mother offered herself to me to pay your father's debt."

"Liar!" Zenna dragged herself to her feet, using the worktable as a crutch. She took a step toward him, her arm dropping to her side. Her fingers brushed over the leather sheath, dipped under her hem, and curled around the knife handle.

Mother's gaze flicked to her hand. He clucked his tongue. "That would not be a wise choice."

He waved his hand and vanished. Zenna spun around, her frantic gaze searching the tower for movement. Where had Mother gone? She pulled the knife out and held it up in front of her chest.

"Terrifying, isn't it?" Mother's deep voice purred. He wrapped his arm around her torso, crushing her back to his chest. Cold metal pressed into her throat.

"What is?" She stiffened, her heart hammering. The scent of gasoline overwhelmed her.

"Knowing how close you are to death… now, drop the knife."

It clattered to the ground.

"Good." He loosened his grip, moving his knife away from her throat. Dragging the sharp point down the side of her face, it scratched her skin but did not draw blood. "Do you want to know why I chose you?"

She sat her teeth into her lower lip and nodded, a barely perceptible movement of her head.

"Your mother was a stunning woman, her coloring quite similar to yours, but she never looked more beautiful than the day she married your father," Mother murmured against her cheek. "Yes, I was there. I stood at your father's side, his best man."

"I don't believe you." Zenna stared at the fireplace, her body numb. How could her parents befriend such a monster?

Mother spun her around, his fingers pinching her chin, jerking it up.

"I've known your father over half my life. He was a talented herbalist, and as luck would have it, he was assigned to my dormitory at university. But he had a gambling problem and ended up owing more than he could pay to a local bookie. We settled on a mutual arrangement—he grew the plant necessary to produce Votras Alute, and I cleared his debts. We continued in this partnership for some time until he met Anna."

Releasing Zenna, Mother strode to the window. He smacked the latch up and shoved the shutters open. Moonlight streamed into the tower.

"She was good for him, your mother. Convinced him to stop gambling, stop drinking. He became more focused, dedicated to his work." Mother spun around. "On my birthday, he presented me with a gift, a new strand of the plant. It was stronger, more potent, less required to make Votras Alute. Enzo planned to seed his land with it, but then, your mother fell ill, and your father, so desperately afraid to lose her,"—derision rolled through Mother's voice—"made an unforgivable choice."

"You took advantage of him." Zenna's hands clenched, and she took a step toward Mother.

"Your father stole from me!" Mother kicked the sofa, and it slid eight feet across the tower. She jumped out of the way, just before it crashed into the worktable, jarring the mortar and pestle. "He cut down my flower and boiled it into a broth, and your greedy mother drank every drop."

"It saved her life." Zenna grabbed the back of the sofa, her legs trembled. "How can you deny true love?"

"True love?" Mother snorted. "The first time I came for my plant, your father fell on his knees before me, a pathetic, whining, blubbering mess of a man, begging me for mercy because of *true love*."

"You should have given it to him."

"I did." Mother stalked toward her. "I gave him five years to recreate a new plant. I lost thousands of dollars—"

"I know." Zenna interrupted him with a grumble. "I've been paying it back."

Ire flashed across his face, and then, a hint of amusement. He reached out and wrapped his hand around the back of her head, jerking her forward.

"When I returned for my plant the second time, your father had been unable to replicate his earlier success. He asked me to spare his life."

"And my mother…"

"Your mother threw herself over his body and pleaded for a different solution." He wrenched Zenna's neck, pulling her forehead against his. "A physical arrangement."

Zenna swallowed.

"She took me into their bedroom, while your father waited outside in the garden, a puddle of misery curled onto a stone bench. She pushed me back on their bed and removed her clothing one piece at a time." He shuddered as the memory rolled over him.

"You cheated on your wife?" Shock dripped from Zenna's voice.

"What do you know of Moira?" Mother frowned and leaned back, releasing her neck.

"I assumed you were with Malik's mother at the time since he's not much older than me." Zenna leaned back against the rear of the sofa and folded her hands in her lap, pasting an innocent look on her face.

"We had an understanding—she looked the other way, and I let her keep her life."

"If you had relations with my mother, why did you kidnap me?"

"I was distracted from completing our arrangement." Mother drew one finger down her arm. Zenna shivered. "As Anna climbed on top of me and began grinding her pelvis against my erection,"—he smirked when Zenna frowned, appalled by his vulgarity—"I heard a soft noise, almost like the voice of an angel. I sat up, shoved your mother off my body, and yanked up my pants. Rising from the bed, I padded into the next room. She chased me, begging that I allow her to finish, but curiosity had diverted my interest. It was you I discovered in the next room, your golden hair surrounding you like a halo. I was disturbed, offended Enzo had failed to disclose your existence to me."

"I'm sure he had good reason to protect his child from a murderer such as yourself."

Mother's hand tightened around her arm, squeezing until she cried out.

"I spared your parents' lives."

"But how many others have you taken?" she asked, jutting out her chin.

"Malik has made you brave," Mother replied. Stepping forward, he pinned her body against the back of the sofa. "I can't say I'm enjoying this new trait of yours."

"Why did you take me?" Zenna repeated the question, a hard edge in her voice.

"You saved my life." Mother tilted his head. "Don't you remember?"

She shook her head.

"Your mother attacked me, struck me from behind with a vase she seized from the windowsill. A piece of the porcelain embedded itself in my skull, and I dropped to the floor, a pool of blood growing underneath my head. Your mother screamed for your father, who raced into the house. While they argued over what to do, you crawled over to me and placed your chubby hand on my face."

Zenna closed her eyes, straining to recall the image, but her mind returned empty memories.

"Rising from the floor, you glanced at your parents, whose heated discussion had evolved into screaming, then toddled over to a dresser. After retrieving a hairbrush, you brought it back to me and plopped down. You laid beside me, your eyes even with mine, and stroked the hairbrush through my hair. A strange warmth flowed through my head, entering at the wound, and traveled through my veins. When your mother realized what you were doing, she snatched you away from me, flinging you over her shoulder. They left all their possessions and ran."

"I should have let you die," Zenna said, her voice barely a whisper. His revelation sent ice sliding down her spine. Her imprisonment was the direct consequence of her compassion.

Mother grinned. "I laid on the floor over twenty-four hours, forcing myself to breathe while your hair slowly healed me. Once I recovered, I tested the hairbrush and discovered the same natural compound that was in the plant was also in your hair. I knew I had to have you."

"How did you find us?" she asked, the question stuck in her throat.

"It took several months of searching, but Moira was a gifted tracker—one of the few attributes she passed on to Malik before her death—and she discovered your parents hiding along the northern coast." Mother glanced to the right, his eyes falling on the mortar. He stepped back and ambled to the worktable. Lifting the pestle, he sifted the green-grey powder.

"When we arrived at the cottage, it was well after midnight. The moon, barely a sliver in the sky, cast no light upon us as we crept around the side of the small hut."

"They didn't hear you?" Zenna took a step toward him, lifting her hand, a chastisement on her tongue.

"Our movements were drowned out by crashing waves." Mother glanced up, surprise flashing across his face as he drank in Zenna's reprimanding stance. He set down the pestle.

"Did Moira know you were going to kidnap me?" she asked, relaxing against the sofa.

Mother frowned. "Why do you ask?"

"As a mother herself, I can't imagine she would condone the theft of a child."

"Moira had one interest in life, Malik. Every choice she made was for him. In the weeks prior to your abduction, she'd had a rather disturbing change of heart and decided this life was no longer for her or her son. We reached an agreement—she helped me retrieve you, and I allowed her and Malik to leave."

"But Malik is still here."

"Was here," Mother corrected her with a dark smile.

"You broke your word to her, too!"

"I did not!" Anger vibrated through the tower. "Once you were hidden away, I released Moira and Malik. They vanished in front of me, melting into the morning sun. I didn't see my son for five years."

"Vanished?" A wrinkled etched itself across Zenna's forehead. "Malik has no magical talents."

"You're correct," Mother replied, an odd tone in his voice as if he were astonished Zenna knew that fact. "However, Moira was a talented sorceress."

"Then—"

"Why am I the only person still alive?" A heavy hand landed on her shoulder and pinched the soft flesh of her neck. She cringed, doubling over at the waist as he squeezed. "Because I am strong."

"How did Malik end up back in your control?" Zenna asked through clenched teeth, unsure she wanted to learn the answer.

"Votras Alute." The words hung in the air. He released her, stalked the length of the tower, and spun at the open window. "Like so many before her, Moira became addicted to the drug. It was Malik who reached out to me, asking for help."

Zenna had heard stories from the men, rumors of people so desperate for the drug, they would trail behind Mother's couriers, offering their souls for a speck of purple dust.

"I didn't recognize her when Malik brought me to her." Mother's mouth pulled into a grimace. "Together, we weaned her off the drug. Gradually, her powers returned."

"Was she grateful?"

Mother snorted. "Grateful that I had tweaked the formula,

making Votras Alute one of the most addictive substances in the country? No, she was not. She pleaded with me to stop producing the drug. When I refused, she vowed to shut down my business."

"So, you killed her?"

"First, I tried to reason with her, but when she discovered I still had you, she threatened to send me to prison... then, I killed her."

"Malik—"

"Never once questioned my decisions," he interrupted with a snarl, "until he met you."

"Have you no feeling?" Zenna asked, horrified at Mother's coldness.

Crossing the room, his hand closed around Zenna's throat and yanked her from the back of the sofa, dangling her over the stone floor. His free hand flew, smacking her across the face, rattling her teeth.

"You have until morning to make a batch to rival the one I collected today." Mother's growl swirled around her. "If you succeed, I will spare your parents' lives, but if you fail, you will witness every minute of suffering I inflict upon them."

He waved his hand and disappeared. Zenna dropped to the floor, gulping down a lungful of oxygen. Her face throbbed, her body ached, but the pain oozing from her heart crippled her. She rolled onto her back, her gaze on the rafters. Mother knew she couldn't produce a full batch in one day. He wanted her to fail.

A shadow swooped into the tower through the open window. She screamed and flung up her hands when it dove at her face. The shadow charged again, screeching as it flew past her head. She scrambled underneath the worktable and peered out, her gaze moving slowly over the tower as she sought her attacker. A peculiar flapping sound came from the rafters. She craned her head, staring up.

"A bird?"

The raven cawed and dove at her again.

8

"Get out!" she yelled and waved her arms at the raven, attempting to shoo it from the tower. Instead, it circled the room once and landed on the back of the sofa, furthest from Zenna, its beady eyes locked on her.

Bending its head, the raven pecked the sofa, poking a small hole in the shabby material. It glanced up as if judging her reaction, then hopped closer. Stopping halfway across the back, it pecked another hole.

"Stop that." She crawled out from underneath the worktable.

The raven tilted its head, considering her command, then bowed its head again, digging a third hole in the sofa.

"Hey!" Zenna took a step toward the bird. It froze, its beak buried halfway in the sofa. "I know it doesn't look like much, but I don't have anything else to sit on, so I would appreciate it if you would stop poking holes in my furniture."

The raven cawed—she assumed in complaint—hopped off the back of the sofa, and landed on the center cushion, where it paced in a tiny circle, flapping its wings. A small piece of parchment wrapped around its ankle, tied with twine, caught her attention.

Curious, Zenna leaned over the back of the sofa, reaching out slowly. Just as her fingers neared the bird's leg, it squawked and jabbed her hand with its sharp beak. She drew back with a gasp, blood gathering on the fleshy part of her hand between her thumb and forefinger, and wrapped her apron around the wound.

"I'm trying to help you." She straightened and glared at the raven. "You flew into my tower."

The raven cawed again, a staccato castigation, and hopped to the far end of the sofa.

She sighed, rolling her eyes. "May I remove the parchment from your leg?"

Tilting its head, the raven locked its gaze on Zenna, then skipped forward and held out its leg.

At a glacial pace, Zenna's trembling fingers neared the bird. The raven did not move. Encouraged, she grabbed one end of the twine, tugged, and the parchment tumbled free from the bird. She snatched the rolled piece of paper from the cushion and unfolded it, smoothing it out on the back of the sofa. Her eyes scanned the scribbled words, then she glanced up at the bird.

"This is a recipe."

The raven cawed.

"What does it make?"

Instead of responding, the raven hopped to the end of the sofa and took flight. It soared around the tower, circling the room twice before returning to the sofa.

"I appreciate your enthusiasm, but I don't understand you," she said, her gaze sliding over the jars of ingredients. Did she have everything written on the parchment?

She walked to the rear wall, her fingertip trailing along the row of unlabeled jars, selected several of the containers, then carried them to her worktable. With the beginning stage of Votras Alute resting in the mortar, she couldn't use the stone bowl to combine the ingredients on the parchment, or she would ruin the batch. She grumbled, her gaze lifted to the bird.

"I hope this is worth the trouble you're causing me."

The bird turned away, jumped down from the sofa, pecked one of the stones in the floor, then glanced over at her.

"Do you think it will work?"

After collecting the jars from the worktable, she scooted around the sofa and set them next to the fireplace, lining them up in order of use. She returned to her worktable and grabbed the pestle, knocking the green-grey powder from its base. A small bit of residue remained on the base of the pestle. She glanced over at the fire crackling in the fireplace.

Holding the pestle in the embers, she burned off the remaining powder, sat on the floor, and smoothed the parchment flat, pinning it open with two jars. The raven took residence on the nearest jar, watching her with interest as she took a large pinch of marigold and ground the plant into dust, adding thistle, then licorice root. The powder took on a glittering black color. A burst of elation exploded from the bird. It hopped off the jar and landed in the center of the pile.

"Shoo." Zenna waved her hand, but the bird ignored her and sunk its beak into the mound.

A screech echoed off the rafters. The raven fluttered madly as the black powder rose from the floor and swirled around it, enclosing the bird in an opaque whirlwind of glittering onyx.

Zenna scrambled backward, her eyes widening. The whirlwind grew larger and lifted the raven, swirling faster and faster as the raven screamed. Covering her ears, Zenna ducked behind the sofa. Feathers exploded from the whirlwind, covering her and the tower with black fluff, which dissolved like mist before the morning sun.

"That was my least favorite experience so far," a deep voice, coated in exhaustion, rumbled.

Zenna peeked out, her gaze landing on a nude figure resting beside the fireplace.

"Malik?"

"In the flesh, as it were." He groaned and sat up.

"Malik!" She leapt over the sofa and dove at him, knocking him onto his back. "I thought you were dead."

"I thought the same thing." He buried his face in her neck, his arms tightening around her and crushing her waist.

She cried out, sinking her teeth into her lower lip. Malik drew away, his face dark. Lifting his hand, he brushed a piece of hair from her face, and hissed. His finger lightly traced the bruise on her cheekbone.

"It's nothing," she said.

"Nothing doesn't make you scream in pain."

"I heal quickly." She stilled his finger, her hand closing around his, and forced a weary smile. "How did you survive your father's wrath?"

"After torturing me unconscious, he transformed me into a raven. I woke in a cage hanging in the prison beneath the center of the compound. He planned to impose a regimented schedule of torment to reprogram me into the son he wanted. My cellmate took pity and released me from the cage. I was able to squeeze through the bars of the upper window and fly away."

"Who was your cellmate?"

"Carlyle."

"Your uncle?" Zenna crawled backward off Malik, numbness flowing through her body. "Mother found him?"

"And punished him as well," Malik said as he sat up again. He did not ask how Zenna came to learn of Carlyle's familial connection to him. "My father broke his legs."

"Why would he do that?" Zenna gasped.

"Because Carlyle betrayed him."

A whimper clawed its way out of Zenna. She and Malik had been foolish to think they could escape Mother's grasp.

"Don't cry." Malik drew her into his lap. "We will beat him."

"How?" She stared up at him through tear-filled eyes. "He's too powerful."

"We have an ally." Malik brushed a kiss across her forehead.

"Carlyle won't be much help," Zenna replied.

"I'm not talking about Carlyle."

"Who else is willing to stand up to your father?"

"My mother."

Zenna's jaw dropped. "She's dead. Mother admitted he killed her."

"Apparently, he didn't do a very good job." A grin flashed over Malik's face. "Carlyle rescued her and hid her in a cave high up on the northern cliffs."

"Why didn't he tell you?"

"Because, like my father, Carlyle believed I was loyal to the family. When he heard I was responsible for the courier attacks, he broke me free of the cage and told me her location. I escaped through the window at the base of the building and flew straight to her. She knew me immediately." Malik smiled, his face glowed. "She was exactly as I remembered... with a few grey hairs."

Zenna chewed her lip. "Why didn't she break your father's spell?"

"My father stripped her powers." Malik sighed, the heavy sound filled with heartache.

"But the parchment, how did she know to give it to you?"

"She can talk to animals, a peculiar gift of hers she attributes to a talisman she wears around her neck. I told her of you. She wrote the ingredients down, tied the note to my leg, and told me to return to you. However, the powder will only transform me into a human until sunrise. After that, I transform back into my feathered form. The only way for the spell to be permanently reversed is to defeat my father, and for that, we need to gather an army."

Zenna extricated herself from his embrace and stood. She paced to the window.

"I can't fight with you."

"Why not?" Malik frowned.

"If I don't produce a full batch of Votras Alute by tomorrow morning, Mother will torture and murder my parents in front of me."

"I will help you complete the batch." Malik climbed unsteadily to his feet. "Our plan has not changed, Zenna. I will find your parents. You will be free."

Zenna nodded as her gaze slid over his body, starting at his chest and moving down over his abdomen. Her tongue glued itself to the roof of her mouth as all manner of erotic thoughts tumbled through her mind.

"What are you thinking about?" Malik asked, his voice tinged with amusement.

"You're naked." Heat colored her face, extending below her shirt.

Malik glanced down and grinned. "So, I am."

"Do you plan to rectify that?"

"Nope." He stretched his arms in an exaggerated pose.

"It's distracting."

"I can think of something more distracting." He crossed the room and enveloped her in his embrace, gently wrapping her in his arms. She sucked in a quick breath, and Malik froze, his eyes searching hers. "I don't want to hurt you."

"You won't," she replied, sliding her hands up his arms.

He bent his head and touched his mouth to her lips. Lightning shot through her veins. She moaned and pressed herself into him, her body thrumming and craving his touch.

Malik's tongue slid into her mouth. His grip tightened, his hard length dug into her. Backing her against the wall, he lifted her, wrapping her legs around his waist, then pushing the hem of her shirt up, Malik thrust into her, driving deep into her center.

She cried out, desire pooling in her stomach, and dug her nails into Malik's shoulders.

His lips moved along her jaw, nipping the sensitive skin and sending shivers ricocheting down her spine. Murmuring his name, she rocked against him, meeting each urgent thrust with her own, her body tingling as if her nerve endings were ablaze with need.

Passion ripped through her, winding the tension in her body tighter and tighter until she could think of nothing but her release. He drove into her relentlessly, bringing her closer to the brink. She tensed, her head tipped back in ecstasy, moans tumbling from her lips. His pace increased to a demanding tempo as he slammed into her.

The orgasm ravished her. Screaming his name, she trembled uncontrollably. He sank into her again, thrusting hard, and released, her name echoing, a deafening sound which overtook her cries. They slid to the floor in a tangle of limbs.

"I'd spend the rest of my life as a bird if I got to do that to you every night," Malik murmured against her skin, sending little shockwaves through her body.

"You may get your wish," she replied with a heavy sigh.

"Why do you say that?" He propped his head on his hand, his gaze bore into her.

"I know where my parents are." She closed her eyes and drew in a shuddering breath as the realization crashed over her. Tears leaked down her cheeks. Zenna wiped the back of her hand across her face and opened her eyes. Her gaze locked on Malik. "Mother took them."

"He told you that?"

She shook her head. "It's the only way he can carry out his threat."

"I don't follow."

"How will Mother kill my parents in front of me? He's not

going to take me anywhere, it's too exposed, too risky. He's going to bring them to the compound."

"Unless… They're already here!" Malik gasped and sat up, his head whipped toward the window. "I've seen them."

"Where?" Happiness exploded in her chest.

"In the prison, in iron birdcages very similar to the one I recently occupied."

"Which cell are they in?" Zenna rose and turned toward the window. They had been less than five hundred feet away for the whole of her life. She placed her hands on the ledge and leaned out, her gaze slid along the base of the building in the center of the compound. Every ten feet in the wall, a break in the foundation appeared, indicated by a small brick archway.

"That one." Malik rumbled in her ear, pointing to the second archway from the left. "This entire time, I thought my father collected rare birds. Apparently, he was collecting people."

Zenna spun around. "What do we do?"

"Do you still have the mirror?" His fingers wrapped around hers, drawing her trembling body against his. She leaned into his warmth.

"It fell under the bed."

"You left it under the bed?" He frowned, a flash of hurt lit his eyes.

"Your father didn't give me much choice." She pulled her hand free and shuffled toward the staircase.

Darkness rolled through the tower. "What else did he do to you?"

"Nothing worse than he's done before." She spoke without turning, then squealed as Malik lifted her from the floor and cradled her against his chest. Pushing against his shoulder, she leaned away, struggling in his embrace. "I can walk, you know, I'm already healing."

"You have informed me of your capabilities; however, I have a limited amount of time with you and would prefer to keep you in my arms as long as possible." He dropped a kiss on her nose, then climbed the staircase, one step at a time.

When he reached the loft, he brushed his lips over hers, his tongue teasing the corner of her mouth. She wove her fingers through his hair, pulling him closer as her lips parted. Malik's grip constricted, his tongue dipped into her mouth. Carrying her to the bed, he laid her down, his body covering hers, then he pushed between her legs, his fingers diving under the hem of her shirt, and dragging it over her hips. His mouth moved across her skin, leaving a trail of kisses along her jaw. Her body arched, grinding against him.

A spark of light, glimmering at the corner of the bed, caught Zenna's attention. She twisted.

"What is that?"

Malik lifted his head from her neck and grimaced. "My mother."

"Your mother?" Zenna's head whipped back and forth, expecting the woman to leap out from the shadows.

He crawled to the side of the bed, shoved his arm between the bed frame and the wall, scraping his fingers across the wooden planks, then jerked his arm up. The small silver disc glistened in his fist.

"While my father was occupied with my punishment, Carlyle filched his mirror. I carried it in my beak for miles. It's the only way to communicate with her." He raised the mirror to his face, his thumb on the clasp.

"Don't you think you should cover up?" Zenna asked, her eyes flicked down.

He smirked and tugged the thin quilt over his waist. "Does that make you more comfortable?" She glowered at him as he popped open the mirror.

"Malik!" The breathy voice exploded from his hand. "What took so long? I was afraid your father had captured you."

A red tinge crept into his face. "To be honest, I was preoccupied."

"I gave you plenty of time for a reunion, Malik. You should have been less... preoccupied."

"I was distracted a second time."

"A second time?" Curiosity dripped from her voice. "May I see her?"

Malik passed Zenna the mirror. She took a deep breath and turned it around to face her. A woman, her long black hair interspersed with silver strands, stared through the glass, her stoic gaze a duplicate of Malik's.

"So, you are the girl who has given my son back his heart." Moira's musical voice rang in the loft. "I owe you a great debt. I thought Malik was lost forever the day his father took me from him, but you have brought him back to me. There is no way to repay that kindness. It would be my pleasure to call you my daughter."

"I didn't propose." Malik pressed against Zenna's shoulder, his face squeezing into view.

"Why not?" Moira's eyes flicked to him. "You love her, don't you?"

"People don't get married before knowing each other longer than a day."

"Again, why not?" Moira asked.

"It's not practical."

"That is your father speaking." Pressing her lips together, Moira glowered at him.

"My mother is a romantic," Malik murmured in Zenna's ear. His lips brushed over her earlobe, sending a cascade of shivers rippling down her back.

"Your fiancée is too," Moira needled him.

"She's not my fiancée," Malik said

"Yet," Moira replied.

"Can we rescue Zenna before we plan the wedding?" Malik growled.

"So, you admit there will be a wedding?" Moira's eyes sparkled.

"I'm not admitting anything." Malik folded his arms across his chest.

"Before you escape, I ask that you free your Uncle Carlyle," Moira said, effectively ending the discussion. "I'm not certain how he fell out of favor with your father, but I heard he was trapped in the underground prison as well."

"Zenna healed his leg."

Moira arched a black eyebrow, her gaze slid to Zenna.

"Without request for compensation?"

"He was in pain," Zenna replied.

"Interesting." Moira drew out the word. "Carlyle owes you favor."

"Did he not repay it when he sent Malik to you?" Zenna asked.

"The two are not connected." Moira's eyes flicked back to Malik. "Carlyle will help you overthrow him."

"Must you kill your father?" Zenna asked, her voice faint. She placed her hand on Malik's arm.

Malik nodded once, his jaw set.

"As long as there is breath in that man's body, he will hunt you until you die from exhaustion. He will hunt us all." Moira's face softened. "Zenna, you have been braver than I ever thought possible, especially for a child as young as you were. I ask you to be brave a bit longer. Can you do that?"

"Yes." Zenna's voice cracked.

"Tell me what you learned." The harsh edge in Moira's voice returned as she shifted her attention to Malik.

"Her parents are being held in the underground prison. They're in birdcages like I was."

"Once you transform back into a raven, fly into their cell, and peck the locks open. Then, lead them to me. After Zenna's parents are safe, you can return for her, then..." A dark smile graced her lips.

"How will I know which ones to open?" Malik asked.

Moira opened her mouth and paused, a faint line etched across her forehead.

"How many are there?"

"Fifteen cages."

"Bring them all. If he has reason for keeping them, we need to find out who they are. The more supporters we have, the better." Moira tucked a strand of hair behind her ear, revealing a long, puckered scar down the side of her face.

Zenna gasped.

Moira's eyes flicked to Zenna. "He's not a gentle man."

"I know," Zenna replied. Moira's mouth pressed so thin, it nearly disappeared.

"Did he touch you?" she growled.

"Only to beat me," Zenna said. She glanced down at her lap. Malik wrapped his arm over her shoulders and drew her close, resting his chin on top of her head.

"He will never hurt you again."

"Please don't promise me something you can't fulfill." She lifted her eyes to his.

"There are only two possible outcomes." Malik cupped her face, his thumb grazed her lower lip. "Either he dies, or I do."

9

"There has to be another solution." Zenna pushed away from him, her gaze seeking Moira, but she had disappeared, and dark fog swirled in the mirror. "Where did she go?"

"She knows the consequences of my actions; the only person I have to convince is you." Malik folded her fingers over, closing the mirror, and extracted it from her hand.

"I don't want you to die." She turned toward him.

"I don't intend to."

"But—"

He placed a finger over her mouth.

"I know who my father is, and I know what he is capable of doing." Malik leaned forward and pressed his lips to hers, stealing her breath. When he pulled away, his eyes glowed with a fierce light. "I refuse to become him."

Zenna nodded and bit her lip, blinking rapidly to keep the tears from sliding down her face. Was this the last time she would see Malik alive? Her heart stuttered, thudding painfully. Twisting away, she pressed her palms to her eyes. Malik's hands wrapped around her wrists and pulled her arms down. Brushing the pad of his thumb underneath her eyes, he gathered the tears that formed.

"He won't spare your life a second time," she said, swallowing a sob.

"You would stay with my father to save me?"

"I would."

"Zenna," he sighed her name and drew her against his chest, stroking his fingers through her hair. "You don't know what you're agreeing to do."

"An eternity of servitude is worth your life," she mumbled against his skin.

"My father has disowned me, left me to die in prison, forever trapped in a small iron cage." He lifted her chin. "He has no successor… where do you think he will get one?"

"No." Horror spread through Zenna. "I refuse."

"It won't be by choice." Malik's face darkened. "And if the child you bear him possesses the same unique attributes as you…"

"Is that why he was with your mother? He was hoping you would retain some of her magical capabilities?"

"I was a great disappointment." Malik grimaced. "But as his only child, he showed patience for us both for several years. However, he grew tired of waiting and threatened to kill me if my mother did not produce a more capable heir. She failed. To appease his anger, she performed a spell to transfer some of her abilities to him."

"Why didn't she just take you and leave?"

"My mother has never admitted how she ended up with my father or why she had to barter for our freedom, and I have never pressed her for the answer. It was a dark time in her life she does not discuss. Carlyle told me once when he was inebriated, she was a gift from Bruno Rossi. My father was not gentle with her."

"Did she ever love your father?" Zenna asked.

"Would you?" Malik tilted his head.

"No." She fell silent, her fingers picking at a loose thread on the edge of the quilt. His hand covered hers and squeezed gently.

"You don't have to stay with me."

Her head whipped up. "I don't understand."

"Once you're free, you can go anywhere, do anything you like. There is no obligation between us."

"I thought you wanted to marry me."

He laughed. "I do, but I want it to be your choice, not because you believe you owe me a debt."

She chewed her lower lip. "Can we live near the ocean?"

"We can live wherever you like." He wrapped her in his arms and dragged her against his side, touching a gentle kiss to her temple. "Now, before you sidetrack me again,"—she grinned —"we need to finish the vials. For our plan to work, my father must not suspect anything tomorrow."

"Have you ever made Votras Alute?" Zenna asked, climbing from the bed. Her body complained, reluctant to leave the warmth of Malik's arms.

"No, but I'm a quick learner." He wiggled his eyebrows. "Tell me what to do, and I'll do it."

"You sound like an exemplary soldier."

"I was."

"What happened?"

"My king betrayed me." He rose from the bed, pulling free of the quilt. Zenna's gaze dropped, and her stomach clenched. She blushed, heat crawling through her face, and spun around, her back to Malik.

"I don't have anything you can wear."

He snickered. Rustling followed, then the sound of cloth rubbing cloth.

"Will this subdue your distraction?"

She turned and giggled as Malik spread his arms wide and bowed. The ragged quilt hugged his body, wrapped around his waist, and curved over his shoulder, the excess material trailing down his back.

"That's interesting."

"Step one, don't distract the chemist." He winked. Sliding forward, he took her hand and raised it to her lips. "Step two?"

"Check the batch." She indicated the tower behind her. "Can you move the sofa back? It will be difficult to work with it smashed against my table."

"I am at your service." He brushed his mouth across her knuckles, his eyes blazing. Leading her down the staircase, he stopped at the window, and his gaze flicked over the shutters. "Step two, secure the perimeter." He released her hand.

"Let me." She stopped him, her hand pressed against his chest. "Only one person should lean out that window. If Mother is watching…"

Malik's eyes flicked down to his chest.

"One of these steps had better be to seduce the chemist."

"It follows. Fill all the vials," she replied as desire flooded her body.

"How soon until we get to that step?"

Backing her into the wall, Malik's hands slid down her arms, his fingers drawing sensual trails over her skin, then closed around her wrists. He lifted them over her head and pinned her against the rough stone, his mouth hovered millimeters from hers.

Her breath caught.

"Stop?" Malik asked, his eyes blazing.

She shook her head.

Releasing her wrists, he grabbed her butt, lifted her, and pushed her against the wall. His mouth claimed hers as his hips ground into her.

She tore at the quilt, ripping it from his shoulder, her fingernails digging into his skin, her body begging for release.

"Step one," she managed to grind out through the scorching passion raging through her veins.

With a groan, Malik set her down, sliding her the length of his body, then moved away from her, taking one rather large step backward. Adjusting the quilt, he tightened the wrap—an action that accentuated his arousal—and flung the excess portion over his shoulder, then lifted his gaze, his face expressionless.

"Don't distract the chemist," he growled.

Inhaling a shaky breath, Zenna turned and leaned out the window. She could feel the heat rolling off Malik. Ignoring the fluttering in her stomach, she pulled each shutter closed and latched them together. When she spun around again, Malik stood directly behind her. She gasped.

"Please don't be angry with me," she said, her voice faltered as her eyes dropped.

"I am not your captor." Malik lifted her chin. "Nothing you do will upset me. And after we're free of my father, I'll have plenty of time to dedicate to seduction." Leaning forward, he brushed a chaste kiss across her mouth. "I do like hearing my name on your lips."

Zenna swallowed and nodded. She wobbled toward the worktable on unsteady legs, Malik trailed behind her. A blush lingered just below her skin, warming her body. Retrieving the final jar from the back wall, she unscrewed the lid, and the acrid smell of decay assaulted her. Removing one piece, she smashed the lid back on and wrenched it tightly.

"What is that?" Malik asked, glancing up from the arm of the sofa, where he perched. His nose wrinkled.

"Dried lizard tail."

Malik paled, his face taking on a greyish color.

"Lizard and human hair? Why do people ingest that stuff?"

"I doubt your father tells his customers the ingredients." Zenna dropped the tail into the mortar. "Hold your breath for a moment."

Sucking in a quick breath, Zenna smashed the tail into pieces with the pestle. She ground the sections into smaller chunks, pulverizing them into powder, then exhaled, indicating Malik to do the same.

Malik inhaled and gagged. "That's like rotten eggs mixed with burned motor oil."

"The smell will dissipate with the next ingredient." She spun on the stool and gave him a half-smile. "I just have to find where I dropped the knife."

"It's there." Malik ambled around the sofa and retrieved the knife from underneath the shelves. He held it out with a grin. "Now, you're armed again."

She laughed and accepted the knife, rising from the stool. Following her hair through the tower, she wandered up the staircase and sank onto the bed. She grabbed a section of hair, measuring two-and-a-half inches from the end, and sliced the knife through the strands. As she slid the knife back into the sheath, she noticed the mirror flash.

"Malik?" she asked, forcing her tone to remain even.

"What?" His voice echoed from beneath the staircase.

"The mirror is glowing again."

"Don't open it!" He appeared in the loft, huffing, and snatched up the mirror. After climbing onto the bed, he scrambled to the corner of the mattress and shoved the mirror between the bed and the wall, and it hit the floor with a dull thud.

"What if it's—"

"There's no one for whom you need to answer that mirror."

"Do you think it's your father?" Zenna asked, her chest constricted.

"I don't know, but I'm not willing to find out." Malik crawled to her, swung his legs around, dangling them over the side of the bed, and leaned into her shoulder. "Swear to me, you will not reopen the mirror."

"I promise."

"Good. Now, are you ready to put pieces of yourself in the bowl?"

"It sounds disgusting when you say it that way." Zella's fingers closed around the strands of hair in her palm and glanced at the foot of the bed. Who was on the other side of the mirror?

"I cannot think of a less disturbing description." He rose and held out his hand. "Sunrise is coming. If we're going to pull off this plan, we need to finish those bottles before I become a bird again."

Zella nodded and stood, taking his hand

"I hope your muscles are sturdy. Once I add my hair, the powder has to be ground until it turns deep purple."

"How long does that take?" he asked, descending the staircase behind her.

"It depends on several factors." She shrugged. "Each batch is different."

"Don't you follow the same recipe every time?"

"Of course, but I'm including a varying ingredient. The section of hair added to the formula influences the quality of the drug. The more traumatic the experience that occurred while my hair was growing, the longer it takes the powder to form." She sank onto the stool and lifted the pestle.

"I assume most of your interactions with my father were traumatic."

"They were."

His gaze flicked to her hand, which hovered over the mortar.

"How long ago was the experience you're holding?"

"About a year and a half ago." Zenna sprinkled the hair on top of the green-grey powder.

"What happened during that time?" he asked, returning to the arm of the sofa.

"My birthday." She grimaced and smashed the pestle against the bottom of the mortar. Her wrist automatically resumed the grinding motion, years of muscle memory built into her hands.

She ground silently. Ten minutes passed. She glanced back at Malik, who remained immobile on the sofa.

"Do you want to try?"

"You'll have to show me how." He rose, grabbed a cushion from the sofa, and tossed it onto the floor directly behind her stool. Kneeling, he slid his hands down her arms, over her wrists, and wrapped his fingers around hers. His hands moved in unison with hers. Leaning forward, his mouth touched her ear. "Like this?"

A shiver rolled down her spine. "Yes."

"Tell me about your birthday." His deep voice rumbled in her ear, sending a cascade of tremors rippling down her spine.

She withdrew her hands from the pestle and dropped them to her sides. Warmth curled through her body, the soothing result of Malik's skin rhythmically rubbing against her arms.

"It was the first one I ever had." She spoke to the mortar, watching the green color fade, and the powder took on a slight lavender tinge. "Mother appeared in my tower that morning, holding a large burlap sack. He flung it at my feet and announced he discovered it was my birthday."

"What did he give you?"

She stiffened, the long-buried memory flaring from her subconscious.

"Peaches."

Malik froze. "Why would he give you peaches?"

"They were filled with Votras Alute." She felt the muscles in Malik's arms tighten.

"Is this why you know the powder doesn't work on you?"

She nodded, sinking teeth into her lower lip to hold in a sob as she shuddered. He leaned his head against hers in a comforting gesture.

"Mother said it was a special birthday present, one that would make up for the previous years' oversights."

"He expected a bag of fruit to compensate for years of

neglect?" Malik asked as Zenna guided his hand to the side of the mortar. She knocked the pestle on the edge of the stone and indicated for him to resume grinding.

"I'd never had a peach before," she replied, her tone heavy as the past surrounded her. "I thought it was a gift… but it only took one bite. The amount of Votras Alute in the peach was equal to four vials."

"What happened?"

"I collapsed, convulsing on the floor. Mother stood over me, his laughter echoing around the tower, growing louder and louder until I passed out. When I awoke, I was bound and gagged on the sofa."

"Where was my father?"

"Sitting beside me." Another tremor rolled through her. "He drew my head onto his lap and removed the handkerchief. I tried to sit up, but his hand slammed into my chest. Before I could speak, he shoved half a peach into my mouth and clamped his other hand over my face. He refused to let me breathe until I swallowed the fruit."

She fell silent, lost in the recollection—Mother's acrid scent in her nostrils, the taste of his skin on her tongue, revulsion rolling through her as Mother's hand slid over her chest, down her body, and pressed into her abdomen, restraining her against the sofa as wave after wave of tremors assaulted her. Malik's arms wrapped around her, breaking the trance.

Reaching beneath her hair, she pulled a stark white strand over her shoulder and wound it around her finger. "This is what happens when I use the drug."

"Is it dead?"

"Yes. Mother was ecstatic when the strand changed color. He managed to shove three peaches down my throat before the transformation occurred. He cut a portion of the white piece to make a new batch. The hair caught fire within seconds and disintegrated, leaving a small pile of ash in his palm." She flinched when Malik touched the tress. "Mother beat me until I vomited out the peaches."

"Only this section transformed?"

"Over the next few days, I pulled out the other strands before Mother noticed." Zenna's gaze dropped to the lavender powder. "He hoped ingesting Votras Alute would make my hair more powerful. Instead, it stripped all its healing capabilities. Mother took the remaining peaches and left me on the floor, bound, bleeding, and throbbing in pain."

"I'm sorry." Malik murmured against the back of her head. "I wish I had known about you earlier."

"Thus, the reason he hid my existence from you and everyone else." She twisted around and placed one hand on his cheek. "Mother's cruelty is not your fault, you are not responsible for his actions."

"But I will be responsible for his demise." Malik's face hardened. Picking up the pestle again, he attacked the powder, his vicious grinding pulverizing the remaining chunks in the mortar. Beneath the dull edge of the pestle, the drug transformed, illuminating the bowl in glittering deep purple.

"Stop," Zenna said, detangling the pestle from Malik's cramped fingers.

"Is it done?" He peered over her shoulder.

She nodded. "Would you like to test it?"

"No." Malik climbed from the cushion, rubbed his legs, and stomped across the floor, working the feeling back into his muscles. Birds chirped outside the window. Malik turned, his mouth pulled into a grimace.

"It's almost sunrise."

"All that's left is to fill the vials." Zenna rose and walked to him. She embraced him, sliding her arms beneath his. "Concentrate on freeing the others. I can finish before your father arrives."

"I will return for you." Malik craned his neck and pressed his mouth to hers.

Extricating himself from her embrace, he guided her to the sofa and backed ten feet away. As the sun crested the mountains, sunlight filtered through the shutters, striking him in the back. He cried out and imploded in a burst of black smoke.

Zenna screamed, running toward him. As the smoke cleared, a small, winged shape appeared, hopping in a small circle, its wings flapping against the stone floor.

"Malik?"

The raven cawed in response and took flight, winging around the tower, its voice reverberated off the walls.

She dashed to the window, unlatched the shutters, and pushed them open. Malik circled her once, playfully diving at her head as if to say goodbye, then flew out the window, heading for the prison window.

He landed on the courtyard and toddled forward to the archway. As he reached the alcove, he turned and called out, his caw echoing across the empty courtyard. Behind him, a pair of hands appeared, reaching through the bars, and snatched him from sight.

Zenna clamped her hand over her mouth, her heart pounded with fear. Had Mother captured Malik? Her gaze slid to the staircase... and the mirror. Malik had said not to touch it, but if something happened to him, shouldn't she inform Moira?

What if Mother answered instead? She gulped. Without the vials completed, attracting Mother's attention too early would certainly result in his exacting a horrific punishment on her or her parents.

She hesitated, hovering in the window. A faint caw floated across the courtyard, breaking the early morning silence. She cupped her hands around her eyes, her gaze locked on the archway. Fluttering in the alcove, one black wing appeared—a message from Malik—and vanished.

Relief flowed through her. She grabbed the quilt from the floor and tossed it on the sofa as she floated to the wall of shelves. She selected the first bundle of vials and tucked them into her apron pocket, her gaze flicking back to the window.

"Good luck," she whispered, sinking into the stool, and lifting the metal spoon from its hook. Dipping the spoon into the mortar, she scraped the sides of the stone bowl and filled the first vial.

"I'm pleased to find you working. I was afraid some other distraction had prevented you from your task."

Zenna shrieked and twisted sideways. Mother stepped from the shadows beneath the staircase, his mouth pulled into a sour smile. His dark gaze flicked to the open shutters, then returned to her, asking a silent question.

"There's not enough light in the tower," she replied, using her previous lie, and filled the second vial.

He nodded and trudged to the shelves, walking between the sofa and the worktable. His lips pressed into a thin line.

"I didn't expect you at sunrise," Zenna said, filling another vial. She held it out to him. "Would you like to sample this batch?"

His eyes flicked down and narrowed. "No."

"How will you know if it's potent?" Her forehead wrinkled. Mother never refused a test bottle.

He stroked his fingers over his chin, his dark gaze on the outstretched bottle. His left arm whipped forward, and his fingers closed around the vial. Jerking his arm back, he waved his right hand in a small circle. A bare-chested man materialized in the tower, his body bent into a permanent 'C.' One chain stretched from the iron collar around the man's neck, through the shackles on his wrists, and ended at the cuffs on his ankles. Blood and sweat dripped off his tanned skin.

"You remember Carlyle." Mother strode forward and slapped a hand across the man's back. Not one sound came from Carlyle, save a raspy wheeze in his chest.

"We haven't been properly introduced," Zenna replied, her gaze sliding to Carlyle. He refused to raise his eyes to hers. Dread settled in her stomach. What was Mother planning?

"Carlyle has generously volunteered to test every batch of Votras Alute you produce." With the edge of his thumb, Mother popped the stopper from the vial, wrenched Carlyle's head up, dumped the powder down Carlyle's throat, and flung him away. Falling to his side, Carlyle coughed, spraying blood droplets across the floor. He gasped, the rattling in his chest eased, and he drew in a deep breath.

"Congratulations." Mother sneered, setting his boot on Carlyle's knee. "You didn't kill him."

Mother glared at Zenna, holding her gaze, a dark smile flitted across his face, then smashed his foot to the stones, shattering Carlyle's leg with a nauseating crunch. Carlyle groaned, his teeth grinding together, and vanished. The only indication of his presence was a small pool of blood near the sofa.

"Why did you do that?" Her gaze flicked between the crimson stain and Mother's gleeful face.

"Compassion for a lesser creature?" He laughed, the harsh sound echoed in Zenna's mind. "I can assure you, Carlyle would feel no such thing for you."

"I don't care, I am not a monster."

Mother yanked her from the stool, his fingers constricting around her throat, and slammed her onto the sofa, pinning her beneath his bulk. She kicked her legs but could not throw Mother off her body.

"Who moved the sofa?" He snarled, his face an inch from hers.

"I did." She snapped her teeth at his nose, but he didn't flinch. Instead, his fingers crushed her throat, pushing down until black spots danced in front of Zenna's eyes. She clawed at him, gouging a chunk out of his hand. He hissed and lifted his finger to his mouth, sucking on his knuckle. When he removed the digit, blood gathered in an open wound. He grinned, and terror rolled through her body.

Grasping her wrists, he anchored them above her head with his free hand. Leaning forward, he dragged his cut knuckle over her lips, staining her skin with blood.

"I asked you a question."

"I gave you an answer." She shuddered, jerking her face away. Mother grabbed her face, pinching it between his thumb and forefinger.

"It was not the one I wanted to hear," Mother whispered, the hairs of his beard scratching her chin. His tongue flicked out, touching her cheek. He licked a slow trail up her face. "You're not strong enough to push it out of the way. Who helped you?"

"No one."

"Liar!" Mother's hand whipped across her face. She cried out as pain exploded in her jaw, her body twitched. A dark shadow crossed Mother's face. He reached between them, his hand sliding intimately down her body. "I'm going to enjoy extracting the truth from you."

A loud caw echoed in the tower. The raven soared through the open window, aiming for his father's head. Mother yelled and rolled to the side, falling to the floor with a grunt. Malik dove a second time, his sharp beak sliced a long gash across Mother's forehead.

Zenna scrambled from the sofa, dashed around the worktable, and knelt. Yanking her knife from the sheath strapped to her thigh, she raised the weapon and pointed it at Mother's undulating form.

"What the hell!" Climbing to his feet, Mother swung his fists at the raven as it plummeted from the rafters. It avoided his arms, left a gash in his cheek—underlining his right eye—and cut a hard turn in front of the window. Malik ascended, level with the loft before he descended again for a second attack. Mother covered his head and ducked, cursing at the bird.

Landing on the edge of the mortar, the raven cawed and pecked the bowl, its sharp beak chiseling a piece from the side. The chunk fell to the worktable with a clink, and Mother's eyes narrowed.

"Malik, I'm surprised at your tenacity." He waved his hand, drawing an intricate design in the air. "Speak."

"Don't touch her!" Malik's deep voice rolled through the room, emanating from the raven.

"She is not your concern."

"I love her."

Mother snorted. "Love has made you weak. What has it done for you... cursed to be a bird for the rest of your life?"

"Any curse I suffer from is due to my vindictive father." Malik snapped his beak.

"Careful, Malik. I have been generous with you until now. You don't want to see my bad side." Mother took a step toward the worktable. "How did you get out of your cage?"

"I pecked the lock."

"Clever." A note of pride swelled in Mother's voice. His gaze swept over the tower, and blackness seeped into his eyes when he discovered Zenna crouched behind the worktable, her knife drawn. He snapped his fingers and pointed at the spot directly in front of him.

Zenna rose, set the knife beside the mortar, and approached Mother, each hesitant step on a wave of fear. She paused in front of her stool and swallowed.

"Closer."

Nodding, Zenna inched closer. Mother's hand whipped out, clamped down on her wrist, yanked her to him, then spun her around to face Malik. Crossing his arm over her chest, he pinned her body to his and pressed a rough kiss to her temple.

"Was she worth it, Malik? If I fucked her, would I give up my kingdom too?"

Malik shot off the mortar, flying straight at Mother's face, a black dart of anger. Flinging Zenna aside, Mother swung his arm down and connected with Malik's body. Malik crashed to the floor and skidded across the stones, coming to rest underneath the shelves.

Mother plucked him off the floor, his fist closing around Malik's slight frame, and lumbered across the tower. Collapsing on the sofa, Mother patted the cushion next to him. Zenna shook her head. Mother arched an eyebrow and squeezed Malik, and an anguished caw exploded from his beak.

"Stop it!" Zenna darted forward.

"Sit."

Perching on the farthest side of the cushion, Zenna folded her hands in her lap, her eyes on the raven. Mother loosened his grip and pried on wing free, stretching it out.

"Now, I'm going to ask you a few questions, and if I don't like your answers, I'm going to pluck out a feather."

"Please, no!" Zenna leaned forward, her hand halfway across the sofa before she realized her action. She leaned back and dropped her hand. Mother grinned. He pinched a feather between his fingers.

"What did Malik promise you?" Mother asked, his black eyes on Zenna.

"I asked her to marry me," Malik replied.

Mother glanced down and frowned. "Marry you? You're engaged to Tessa."

"You made that arrangement, I never agreed to the union."

"And where will you and your lovely bride live... in the tower? She owes me quite a debt, and I have no intention of freeing her before that obligation is settled."

"She's paid her debt," Malik said, a hard edge in his voice. "As a wedding gift, let this go."

"Let it go!" Mother leapt to his feet, Malik gripped tightly in his fist, and strode to the window. "What do you think pays for all of this?"

"We have enough."

"It's never enough!" Spit flew from Mother's mouth. His wild eyes landed on Zenna, and a horrifying grin appeared on his face. "I'll make you an offer Malik, one which will return you to your human form and allow you both to have your happily ever after."

"Which is?"

"I want your first-born child."

"Never!" Zenna pushed off the sofa and crossed her arms over her chest. "I refuse."

Mother launched across the room, releasing Malik in his rush to reach Zenna. He backed her against the worktable, his finger gouging her chest.

"You have no say in this matter. Your only decision is whether the child will be Malik's or mine."

"Let her go," Malik said, landing on top of Mother's head. "Back away, or I will peck your eyes out."

"I've had enough of this fairytale bullshit." Mother snatched Malik from his head, separated one wing from his body, and crumpled the wing in his fist, the tiny bones cracking beneath his fingers. Zenna screamed, but her voice was drowned out by Malik's cries of anguish. Prying apart the second wing, Mother repeated his previous action, crushing the bones. "Is there anything you wish to say to your true love before I throw you to your death?"

"Nothing holds you to this place," Malik said, his voice laced with pain.

She nodded, understanding his message. *Her parents were free.*

Mother spun and whipped his arm forward, flinging Malik through the window. Zenna ran across the tower and leaned out. Malik plummeted, his broken wings unable to prevent his raven body from smashing into the harsh ground beneath the tower. Placing his hand on her back, Mother's fingers closed around her shirt and pulled her back into the tower, shoving her toward the shelves.

"You have work to do."

Walking to the worktable, her spine ramrod straight, Zenna lifted the mortar from the table. She spun around, returned to the window, and offered Mother a giant smile. Mother's eyes narrowed.

Before Mother could react, Zenna hefted the mortar out the

window. It tumbled to the ground, hitting the stones with a resounding crash, and deep purple powder exploded across the compound, glistening in the morning sun.

"What did you do?" Mother shrieked. He lifted Zenna by her shirt and thrust her out the window. She dangled above the courtyard, her hands hanging loosely at her sides. She glanced down, her heart pounding.

"Do it," she needled. "Drop me."

With a snarl, Mother yanked her through the window and flung her across the tower. She smashed into the sofa, knocking the oxygen from her lungs, and collapsed backward onto the floor. Mother's heavy boots echoed. He wrapped his hands through her hair and jerked her head up as blood streamed down her chin.

"I can do this all day."

"Every bruise you give me will delay your production." She glared at him, unblinking.

"Your parents will pay for your insolence."

"Tell them I said hello."

Her head crashed back to the floor, and Mother vanished. An angry howl rose from the prison window. Within seconds, Mother reappeared, his hand reclaiming his painful hold on her head.

"Where are they?" Mother struck Zenna across the face, and pain detonated in her head.

"Malik hid them," she replied, a smirk stretching her lips. "And that secret died with him."

A snarl vibrated in Mother's throat. "Malik is not the only one with talents."

"Then find them," she glowered, a dare hovering in her retort. "Until you do, I refuse to make more Votras Alute."

Mother struck her again, and stars exploded behind her eyes. Blow after blow rained down on her body until she collapsed on the floor, her eyes rolling back in her head, Mother's contorted face was the last image she saw before she lost consciousness.

Cold seeped into her skin. She opened one eye, her gaze sliding over the tower. Where was Mother? Opening the other eye, she winced, and her limbs throbbed. How long had Mother stayed to punish her after she passed out?

She rolled onto her side, the ginger movement drawing a hiss to her lips, followed by a sob as the realization of Mother's actions washed over her. Malik was dead, thrown from the tower with broken wings, his shattered body discarded somewhere in the courtyard. She bawled, her misery echoing tauntingly off the rafters. Without Malik's influence, neither Carlyle nor Moira would assist her. She was on her own, but it was only a matter of time before Mother returned from his futile hunt for her parents. With failure as his motivation, Zenna knew Mother would revert to a perverse form of torture. She was her only chance of survival.

Struggling to her feet, she hobbled to the worktable and grasped the knife, a hasty plan forming in her mind. She glanced at the mirror, her gaze on the pale, waif-like girl who stared back.

"Nothing holds you to this place," she said.

She gripped her hair at the base of her neck and exhaled. Drawing the blade across her hair, she cut the blond tresses in one quick swipe. Dropping the hair, she stepped forward and shivered as an incredible feeling of weightlessness passed over her.

"Alright, Malik," she spoke as though he were standing beside her. "You said to tie it around the armoire leg."

Gathering the hair, she carted it over to the armoire and wrapped it around the armoire leg twice. Her gaze skipped to the staircase. There was only one thing she wanted from this place. She raced up the stairs and dove onto the bed. Rooting under the pillow, she pulled out the small sack, retrieved her necklace, and fastened the silver chain around her neck.

She hastened down the stairs and gathered her hair. After flinging the hair out the window, she pulled on it, ensuring it was tightly fastened around the armoire. Climbing onto the window ledge, she turned around, her gazing sweeping over the tower, her home for the past twenty years.

Hooking her hands around her hair, she leaned out the window and climbed down the side of the tower. When she reached the end of her hair, she released the golden tresses and dropped to the ground, landing lightly on her feet.

She spun slowly, her eyes drinking in the compound. Everything seemed so small when she was high above the grounds. She knew the only exit was to the north, but running across the open courtyard seemed risky. If she hugged the walls of the compound, she should be able to escape unnoticed.

A faint sound caught her attention. She froze and pressed against the tower. Had someone seen her climb down? Her gaze slid over the courtyard, seeking the sound. It came again from her right, brittle, as though the owner were struggling to breathe. She narrowed her eyes and gasped.

Ducking her head, she raced over to a small clump of grass. Buried in the greenery was the small black body of a raven.

"Malik?" Hope bubbled in her heart. A moan answered her question. "Don't move."

She knelt, dug her hands under his body, lifted him from the ground, and tucked him into her shirt, cradling him against her breast. She didn't have much time. Her eyes flicked back to the tower. Without any Votras Alute to heal him, she would need to make more, and—except for her hair—the ingredients she needed were in the tower.

"I really hope you appreciate what I'm doing for you," she said into her shirt.

Darting back to the tower, Zenna's gaze scanned the courtyard for any signs of Mother or his men. When she reached the tower, she scaled the wall, slowly climbing until she reached the ends of her hair. She grasped the hair, and hauled herself up the side, hand over hand, sweat pouring down her back.

When the top of her head reached the window, she flung her arm up and grabbed hold of the windowsill. Pulling herself up, her feet scraping against the side of the tower, she dragged herself halfway through the window, twisting awkwardly so as not to crush the raven.

"Going somewhere?"

Her head whipped up. Mother vibrated above her as his hand closed around her shirt.

M other yanked her through the window and threw her over his shoulder. She somersaulted, curling her body around Malik to prevent further damage to his small frame, and crashed to the floor.

"Parents or no, you owe me a debt, and I expect you to repay it." He advanced, and tripped over her hair, his eyes flicked down, following the dull river of gold as it wrapped around the armoire leg. Horror crossed his face, and a deep snarl, louder than thunder, rolled around the tower.

"What have you done?"

"I wanted to save him." She scurried backward and crashed into the back wall, jarring the bookshelf.

"Malik? You cut off your hair to rescue my disappointment of a son?" His anger stretched toward her like the long-fingered shadows of afternoon. "How did you plan to heal him without your hair?"

"I have enough hair." She dragged her fingers through her short tresses and gasped as she touched the cold metal of her necklace. How would she explain why she had it?

"For a full batch?" Mother asked. The odd note in his voice sent a shudder rolling down Zenna's spine.

She licked her lips. If she made Mother a new batch, she could pinch enough while filling the vials to save Malik. Mother wouldn't check the apron pocket for residue. Where could she hide Malik and her necklace until then? Her gaze darted over the tower. The loft would be the safest place if only she could get to it.

"Yes," she replied, her voice wavered.

"And I suppose you want to make a deal?" Leaning down, he grabbed a section of her hair, and yanked, winding a coil of ash blonde at his feet.

Before he glanced up, Zenna's hands whipped up to her neck, fumbled with the clasp, unfastened it, and dragged the chain from her throat. She shoved the necklace into the apron pocket as Mother pulled the ends of her hair through the window. When he looked back, impatience marred his face.

"I do." She stepped toward him, her fingers twisted together. The raven shifted, a minute movement that tickled Zenna's skin. She folded her arms across her chest, gently pressing against Malik. "I'll replace the batch I destroyed, just leave me one vial. Please, let me save his life."

"Where is my son?" Mother twisted around, glaring at her.

"He's where he landed after you threw him." She inched forward. Upon reaching the sofa, she leaned over the arm and snatched up Malik's old shirt. She balled up the material and held it in front of her body.

Mother's eyes followed her movement. "If I let you save him, what will you give me?"

"I will stay with you, without complaint, for the remainder of my life."

Malik pecked her, his sharp beak piercing the skin just below her collarbone. She sucked in a sharp breath and shifted her arms, tapping the raven once on its head to communicate, she understood the sacrifice she was making.

"You will do whatever I ask?" Mother's eyes narrowed.

"Yes, Mother." She lowered her eyes and stared at the floor.

"And I suppose you expect me to retrieve Malik and bring him to you?"

"That would be helpful." She peeked at him, gauging his reaction.

He stalked toward her and walked a slow half-circle around her, his gaze sliding over her body. His hand brushed across the back of her neck, skating across her shoulder blades, following the curve of the shirt's low collar.

"You're dirty," he said. His fingers trailed underneath her chin. She kept her eyes on the ground, but he jerked her head up. "I brought you water last night. Where is it?"

She pointed at the burlap sack hanging from the hook. What was Mother going to do?

Mother strode to the hook and lifted the sack. Digging the strings apart, he jerked the leather canteen from inside and dropped the sack on the floor. His dark gaze lifted.

"Put that shirt down."

Nodding, Zenna bent over the sofa arm, her back to Mother. As she leaned forward, she pulled Malik from inside her shirt and covered him in the second shirt, setting the ball carefully on the cushion.

"Stand by the window."

Zenna complied with Mother's barked instruction. Her gaze followed him as he prowled around the sofa, and her breath caught in her throat. His eyes dropped to the crumpled shirt, then returned to her face. He continued his slow pace toward her.

When Mother reached Zenna, he uncapped the leather canteen. Lifting it over Zenna's head, he tipped the canteen and dumped water on her. She cried out, her muscles tightening as the frigid water streamed down her body. When Mother tilted the canteen a second time, Zenna shrieked, twisting away, but Mother grabbed her arm, his fingers digging into her flesh.

Her shirt clung to her skin, the translucent material revealing the curves of her body. Mother's eyes glowed. His finger hooked under the strap of her tank top, dragging it down her arm.

"You should change clothes."

She turned, angling her body toward the sofa, but Mother blocked her. He shook his head slowly.

"I didn't say you could move."

"You told me to change." She frowned.

"That I did." His other hand snapped out, grabbed the second shirt strap, and jerked it down her arm, revealing the swell of her breasts. Dragging his knuckle up her arm, he leaned forward, his mouth hovering an inch from her skin.

Her stomach knotted. She wouldn't be able to fight off Mother should his thoughts take on a more sinister direction. Clearing her throat, she spoke with feigned conviction.

"I'd like some privacy."

"I'm going to enjoy breaking you." Mother said, the tip of his tongue slid into her ear. She shivered, fighting the urge to pull away from him. He flung her toward the sofa. "Change."

She scurried across the room, snatched up the shirt—with Malik hidden inside—and dashed up the staircase before Mother changed his mind. Jerking the partially open curtain across the loft, she set the shirt on the bed, carefully unwrapping the raven.

"Malik?" she whispered. The raven's foot twitched.

"What is the first ingredient you need?" Mother called from beneath the landing.

"A mortar," Zenna replied.

She untied the apron, dropped it onto the bed, and peeled off her wet shirt, laying it on the floor to dry. Pulling the necklace from the apron's pocket, she shoved it under her pillow, leaving it beside the small sack of grapes and cheese.

"I brought that." Mother's voice sounded as though he were standing beside her.

"You did?" She spun around, her hands flying to cover her body. She was alone in the loft. Peering out from behind the curtain, her gaze sought Mother. He stood at her worktable, in front of him a stone mortar, similar in size to the one she smashed.

That's why Mother had been in the tower!

"What next?" He spun around, his eyes bore into her.

"Ginger root." She dove behind the curtain again.

"How much?" he asked, his voice moving along the back wall of the tower.

"One piece, roughly the size of your palm, chopped finely."

Why did Mother want to know the formula? It was his invention, surely, he remembered the recipe. Was it a test? She dragged the new shirt on, marveling at the simplicity of pulling the shirt over her head.

"Then what?"

"A spoonful of thistle." She knelt beside the bed, her head level with Malik, and drew one finger down his back. He opened his beak and clicked once. "Please hold on a bit longer."

Malik clicked his beak again, forcing two words through his broken body. "I will."

"Promise me, no matter what you hear, you won't intervene," she said.

"No."

"Don't make me put you in a cage." She leaned forward and touched her mouth to his feathered head.

"It cannot take that long to change one article of clothing!" Mother's angry voice ripped through the loft.

Zenna popped up, grabbed the apron, and zipped through the curtain.

"Have you added both ingredients?"

"Yes." Mother turned and glared up at her. "The longer you

take, the less time you'll have to save Malik," he hissed as if his own son's name were so distasteful, he regretted having the word in his mouth.

She darted down the staircase, trying the apron strings as she ran, and headed for the worktable. Inspecting the mortar, she poked the mixture.

"Grind it a bit more. It needs to have more grey in the color."

Mother glanced at her. "Are you certain?"

"Do you intend to test this batch on Carlyle?"

"I do." Mother's face melted into a horrifying grin.

"Then, yes. I'm extremely certain."

"And if I were testing this batch on myself?" His growl startled her.

Zenna swallowed, realizing her error too late. "I would have said the same thing."

"Why don't I believe you?" Mother pounced, his thick hand closing around Zenna's throat, and shoved her backward, pinning her against the wall beneath the staircase. His other hand slid down her body, groping. She jerked away.

Mother punched her in the stomach. She doubled over, the air escaping from her lungs in a low grunt. Lifting her face, Mother slapped her. She dropped to her knees, biting back the sob hovering on her lips. He smacked her again, hitting her until she collapsed on the floor, unable to raise her head. Kneeling beside her, Mother reached into the darkness, grabbed a chain, and fastened it to her ankle, then pulled on the chain, testing the strength.

"Now, I believe you said to grind the powder until it became greyer?"

She nodded.

"What did you say?" His fingers wove through her short hair, and he jerked her from the floor.

"Yes." She gasped. Mother flung her head down. It smashed into the stone, scraping the side of her face.

Mother hummed as he stood. He walked to the worktable and dropped onto the stool. He ground the powder silently. After five minutes, he picked up the mortar and tilted it toward Zenna, who remained immobile on the cold floor, pain pulsing through her body.

"Lizard tail," she said before Mother's ire returned.

He rose and returned to the back wall. Selecting the jar of lizard tail, he glanced over at Zenna. "How many?"

"One," she replied, her breath coming in short gasps. "Grind until the powder takes on a lavender tinge."

She wrinkled her nose, the scent of decay assaulting her as Mother unscrewed the top of the jar. He carried the jar to the mortar, selected one tail, and set it atop of the powder. Turning, he saluted her with the jar, dragged it under his nose, and sniffed. A shudder rolled the length of her body.

"You don't like it?" He pulled another tail from the jar and touched it to his face, dragging the tip across his mouth, and blackness seeped into his eyes. "Smells like death."

Unable to tear her eyes from the macabre display, Zenna gagged, dry heaving. Mother bit off a chunk and spat it at her. She curled into a ball, covering her head, and it flew over her and smacked the stone wall behind her. His mocking laugh swirled around her.

"Always so sensitive." He dropped the other piece back into the jar, slammed on the lid, and twisted tightly. "I was able to beat it out of Malik, but you, no matter how many times you crumple at my feet, you remain soft. Even now, with all the anger coursing through your veins—yes, I see it—I know you are incapable of hurting me."

She uncurled, her gaze finding him. "If you believe me harmless, why am I chained up?"

He smiled. "Because my possessions have a tendency to disappear when I don't lock them up."

"I am not a possession."

"You are a debtor. I own you." His words rumbled across the tower. "I can do what I please with you."

Zenna swallowed. She flipped onto her stomach and pushed back onto her knees. Mother arched an eyebrow as she moved into a defensive crouch. He rolled his eyes and returned to the worktable.

"Malik doesn't have an unlimited amount of time," he said, dropping onto the stool. He lifted the pestle and smashed it into the stone bowl.

"It would go faster if you let me do it." Climbing to her feet, two images of Mother danced in front of her eyes, blurring into one. She stumbled back, her hand on her head, and steadied herself against the wall.

"You're in no shape to work." Mother glanced over, a smirk pulling the corner of his mouth.

"Whose fault is that?" Zenna muttered, jerking her foot. The chain rattled.

"Yours." Mother twisted around on the stool. Bending over, he extracted the knife from his boot, flicked his wrist, whipping out the blade, rose, and approached Zenna.

She jerked away from him, her escape prevented by the short chain. Laughing, Mother's hand flew forward and grabbed the back of Zenna's neck. She cringed, kneeling under his weight.

"How much hair do I need?" Mother gathered her short hair in his fist.

Zenna's gaze flicked over to the mountain of grey-lavender powder in the mortar. Mother had not measured the ingredients. "About three inches."

With a nod, Mother yanked her hair up and sliced the knife through her strands. He clumped over to the mortar and held his hand out over the mixture.

"It would be quicker to slice up the pieces into smaller amounts," Zenna said.

Mother glared and tipped his hand. Dragging the knife across his palm, he brushed the strands into the mortar. After setting the knife beside the mortar, Mother's hand closed around the pestle and attacked the mixture.

Minutes crawled by, accompanied only by the sound of stone scraping stone. Zenna shifted, uncomfortable in her kneeling position. She strained, listening for the soft flutter of Malik's wings. Was he still alive? Her eyes shifted back to Mother. Bent over the worktable, his arms moved in a blur, pulverizing the powder.

Deep purple sparkles appeared on his face. He dropped the pestle with a clink and lifted the mortar, tipping it toward Zenna. She nodded once.

"Shall we test it?" he asked. His gruff voice held a note of anticipation. Without waiting for an answer, Mother waved his arm, and Carlyle appeared between them, bound in the same manner as before. He lifted his eyes to Zenna, their dull brown color filled with anguish.

Mother grabbed an empty vial and scraped it over the top of the mortar, collecting a sample. With a sneer, he marched to Carlyle and crouched. He held out the vial, shaking it between his fingers.

"Open your mouth."

Carlyle refused, mashing his lips together. Mother's eyes narrowed. His hand reached behind him, snatching the knife from the worktable. He held up the knife in one hand and the vial in the other as if giving Carlyle the option to choose. Carlyle's eyes slid to the knife, then back to Mother's face, a silent dare.

Snorting, Mother shrugged and shoved the knife between Carlyle's ribs. He grunted and collapsed, blood pouring from the wound. Mother jerked out the knife, dropped it on the floor, and grabbed Carlyle's head, forcing it back. He upended the vial and tapped the end, dumping the full dose into Carlyle's mouth.

While Mother was distracted, Zenna inched forward, her hand slipped out and closed around the discarded knife. Mother's hand landed on top of hers and smashed it to the floor, squeezing until she cried out and released the knife. He shook his head, a disapproving side-to-side movement that meant more pain was coming.

Carlyle groaned, drawing Mother's attention. He twisted back, and one finger traced the fading scar on Carlyle's ribs.

"I don't enjoy punishing you," he said, his eyes on the scar.

"Yes, you do," Carlyle hissed and dragged in a jagged breath.

"You betrayed me," Mother replied. The coldness in his voice rivaled the hatred blazing in his eyes.

"You lied." Pushing up on his elbow, Carlyle glowered. "You told me the injury was permanent."

"It is." Mother stood, lifted his boot, and stomped on Carlyle's knee, grinding it into the stone floor. Carlyle's howl of anguish accompanied the shattering of his bones.

"Please, stop!" Zenna flung herself at Mother. The chain stretched taut and jerked her backward. She crashed to the floor, her hand less than a foot from Carlyle's head.

Mother's hard gaze flicked to her. He waved his hand, and Carlyle disappeared. Kneeling beside Zenna, Mother snatched the knife from the floor, and his hand stroked over her cropped hair.

"You've asked me for a lot of mercy recently." He placed the sharp edge of the knife against her forehead and scraped it backward over her scalp. Tiny pieces of hair fell from her head.

"What are you doing?" she screamed. Mother's grip on her head tightened, and the knife passed over her head again.

"Neither Malik nor Carlyle deserve your compassion." He wrenched her head sideways, and the knife blade scratched across her skin again.

Lifting her chin, he turned her face to the left, inspecting her head. He rose, refolded the knife, and shoved it back into his boot. He strode to the fireplace, selected a burning log from the dying fire, and walked to the armoire. With his eyes on Zenna, he touched the flames to her hair.

Fire zipped through the tower, following the trail of dull gold. She gasped. Nothing remained of her hair except ash. Mother flung the log back into the fireplace as he lumbered to the table. Sliding his arms around the stone base, he lifted the bowl with a grunt.

"Have a pleasant afternoon."

"You promised to help Malik," she said, tears dripped down her cheeks.

"Did I?" Mother spun around, his eyebrow arched. "Think carefully, what did I agree to?"

"You agreed to let me save Malik."

"And once I find him, I'll let you try." His mouth crooked. "In the meantime, I suggest you use the time to make more Votras Alute. Considering his injuries, Malik may need more than one vial."

"How can I?" She touched her scalp, grimacing at the smoothness of the skin beneath her fingers. "You took my hair."

"Yes, that is a problem." Mother tightened his grip on the mortar and disappeared, his maniacal laughter circled around Zenna's head.

Zenna scrambled to her feet and dashed toward the loft. The chain whipped up, grinding against the wooden beam supporting the staircase, and jerked her leg, the unforgiving iron cuff digging into her ankle. Wrapping her hands around the chain, she yanked, but the chain—connected to the wall through thick metal eyebolt—refused to release. Sweat pouring down her face, she yelled his name, the tower echoed with her heartbreak. No sound answered her frantic cry.

A sob ripped through her chest. She was too late, Mother had won. She sank down on the floor, hysteria bubbling through her veins, and drew her legs into her body. Malik was dead.

"I'm so sorry," she whispered.

"Why are you sorry?"

Zenna lifted her tear-stained face and frowned, her gaze sliding over the tower.

"Who's there?"

"Just me." A fluttering sound followed the statement.

"Malik?" She leapt up, her heart thrumming at a rapid pace. A soft scraping came from above her head. Stretching the chain as far as possible, she hopped out from underneath the staircase, her head craned sideways and caught a flash of black.

"You're going to have to catch me," his heavy voice replied.

"I'm right below you." She held out her apron like a safety net and bent backward, arching her body. Without warning, the raven tumbled from the landing above. Zenna darted forward, her apron outstretched and caught Malik as he fell from the loft. She dropped to her knees and lifted the bird from her apron, cradling it in her palms.

"I much preferred my first hiding place," he said, his attempt at humor accompanied by a groan.

"I thought you were dead."

"Fairly close."

"How did you make it to the landing?"

"He hurt you," replied Malik, his voice dark. "I was halfway across the loft before I remembered I was still a bird."

She stroked her thumb over his head in a gentle caress.

"Mother took the full batch with him, I have no Votras Alute to heal you."

"I hate the stuff, anyway." Pain laced his response. A tear slid down Zenna's cheek and landed on his feathers. "I wanted to see you one last time."

"No." Zenna removed her apron, laid it on the floor, and set Malik in the center of it. "I'm not giving up on you."

"Is that a new haircut?" he asked, his voice faint.

"A gift from Mother." She dragged a hand over her scalp, frustration in her fingertips. Her gaze dropped to the stones in front of her. Tiny hairs, barely discernable in the shadows, decorated the flooring. She gasped. How much time had passed?

Malik's breathing labored. "You can still escape."

"How?" she asked, distracted. Her eyes flew over the jars. Could she reach them?

"After I die—"

"That has not been determined yet," Zenna interrupted and

stood. Stretching as far as the chain would allow, Zenna's fingertips brushed over the jar of ginger root. She needed one more inch.

"After I die," Malik repeated, "use my beak to pick the lock and climb down the tower."

She glanced at him. "Can I use it now?"

"You're that impatient to leave me?"

"No." She picked him up. "We're leaving together."

She jammed Malik's sharp beak into the lock and twisted, drawing an inhuman screech from Malik. The lock clicked, and she pried open the cuff, pulled it from her ankle, and threw it at the wall. Gently placing Malik back on the apron, she stroked one finger over his breast.

"Stay with me a bit longer."

Zenna climbed to her feet and dashed to the back wall, collected the three necessary ingredients, grabbed the pestle from her worktable, and zipped back to Malik. Dropping to the floor, she set the jars and pestle around her in a circle and unscrewed each lid.

"You don't have any hair." His breathing hitched.

"I have scraps," she replied and swept the shaved hair into a small pile. "A batch this small won't take a lot of time."

Malik did not reply. His small chest rose and fell, the slow movement comforting Zenna. She took a small pinch of the first two ingredients and ground them against the stone floor. Within seconds they turned the correct color.

"How did you get off the bed?" she asked, her eyes jumping to Malik.

"I used my foot to push myself across the bed," Malik's labored voice replied. "When I reached the edge, I tumbled off the side and landed on your shirt."

Zenna frowned. "I didn't hear you fall."

"You were preoccupied…"

She shivered and glanced at the shadows behind her, fearing

Mother would burst out from beneath the staircase. Fumbling with the next jar, her sweaty hands slid across the lid. She covered the lid with the bottom of her shirt and twisted. Her arms shook, but the lid refused to budge. What had Mother done to the lid?

"Break it." Malik wheezed.

"I have a better idea."

She twisted around, her gaze searched the shadows. Where was the piece Mother spat at her? Crawling over to the wall, she slid her hands along the floor, feeling for the piece until her finger touched something squishy. She shuddered, picked up the lizard tail, and scooted out from under the staircase.

Setting the decaying piece in the center of the powder, she glanced over at Malik, waiting for his chest to rise. After a long moment, it did, and she exhaled, relief washing over her.

Attacking the tail with the pestle, Zenna ground it into dust and combined it with the grey-green mixture. The color changed instantly. She swept her hair into her palm, sprinkled it on top of the powder, and pulverized the mass. She squealed when it changed to deep purple and dropped the pestle.

"Malik."

He did not reply. Her gaze jumped to him—his chest had stopped moving. She yanked him from the apron and shook him. There was no response. Cradling him in the crook of her arm, she pried his beak open, licked her fingertip, and stuck it into the shimmering purple pile. Her breath caught as she touched her finger to his beak, scraping the powder into his mouth.

"Come on, Malik."

Dipping her finger into the pile again, she coated her fingertip with purple, and added a second dose to his mouth, rubbing it over his tongue and waited.

The raven inhaled.

"Disgusting," Malik said, his weary tone filled with revulsion.

"You're alive!" Crushing him to her chest, Malik pecked her

arm, drawing blood. She released him with a gasp, blushed, embarrassed by her exuberance, and set him down in the center of the powder. "You'll need more."

"You sound like my father," Malik grumbled and dunked his beak into the pile. Muffled curse words streamed from his mouth. When he raised his head, a light coating of purple dusted his feathers.

Zenna laughed.

"I love that sound." He hopped over to her knee and bumped her leg with his head, akin to the manner of an affectionate cat. "Now, we need to get you out of here before my father returns."

"I don't have a rope, your father burned my hair." She gestured at the trail of ash. "Would Moira know any spells to turn me into a bird?"

"Maybe." Malik flapped his wings, stretching them wide. "Much better."

"Are you rethinking the benefit of hair and lizard tails?"

"Nope." He took flight, soared around the room twice, and landed on the banister.

"I left the mirror under the bed," she said, grabbing her apron from the floor and tying it around her waist. As she started up the staircase, Malik hopped off the railing and waddled into the loft. When she turned the corner, he was gone.

Scratching came from beneath the bed. A moment later, the glossy tail feather of a raven poked out from the shadows. Dragging the mirror into the center of the floor, Malik pecked the clasp, and the mirror popped open, thick fog eddying through the glass.

"I'd like to speak with my mother," Malik said as Zenna dropped beside him. The mirror glowed.

"Malik? What's wrong?" Moira's worried face appeared in the center of the glass.

"We have a problem." Malik moved aside, allowing Moira to see Zenna.

"What happened?" She gasped, her eyes widened as she drank in Zenna's bald head and fresh bruises.

"Mother took my hair, so I couldn't save Malik's life."

Darkness spilled across Moira's face. "Why did you need to save my son's life?"

"He broke my wings and threw me from the tower," Malik replied, waddling into view. "Zenna cut her hair, climbed down, and found me."

"Why are you back in the tower?"

"It's the only place I know of with the supplies necessary to make Votras Alute," Zenna said, her voice soft. "Mother caught me climbing back in and assumed I was trying to escape. He burned the hair I used as a rope and shaved off the rest."

"If you had no hair to create the drug, how is Malik standing in front of me?" Moira asked, an unreadable expression on her face.

"I scraped up the shavings and made a small batch." Zenna twisted her fingers together.

Moira glanced at Malik. "Still not certain you want to marry her?"

"I'm not proposing as a bird." He snapped his beak. "We have a different problem. We don't have a rope. Do you know a spell that could help us?"

"Not one I'm strong enough to cast from this distance. The powers I lent your father won't return until he is defeated." She tapped her lip with a long fingernail. "Is Carlyle already gone?"

"That's actually another problem." Malik hopped onto Zenna's leg. "He's still in the prison."

"Carlyle has kept me hidden for years, protected me when no one else would. I owe him," Moira replied, her tone harsh. "Imagine what will happen to him if your father discovers I am still alive."

"His legs are broken," Malik said. "I can't carry him from the cell."

"Mother is punishing him for abandoning his post." Zenna leaned forward. "He makes Carlyle test each new batch. After it heals him, Mother breaks his legs again."

"I'd like to say his cruelty surprises me..." Moira's voice trailed off, her eyes glazed over. After a moment, she shook herself and leveled her gaze with them. "Do you have any of the Votras Alute left?"

"There's a small bit on the floor."

"I'm not going to ask why you used the floor," Moira said, her tone amused. "Malik, take the remaining amount to Carlyle. It won't be enough to heal him permanently, but it should allow his bones to mend. Help him escape the prison."

"What about Zenna?" Malik asked. He hopped off her leg and walked toward the mirror.

Moira's eyes flicked to Zenna. "Do you have anything you can shred into long strips?"

"Like the curtain?" Zenna frowned and glanced behind her.

"Perfect. Rip it apart and fasten the ends together. Once Malik returns from freeing Carlyle, climb down the tower." Moira glanced at Malik. "You'll need to create a distraction to give her time to escape."

"Like an explosion?" Malik asked.

Moira's mouth twitched. "What are you thinking?"

"The western tower stores all the vials of Votras Alute." Malik turned toward Zenna. "Wait until you hear the siren, then climb down. All the men will be occupied with the tower."

"Malik, I appreciate your enthusiasm, but how will you set it on fire? You are limited by your size," Moira said.

"He can add licorice root. It has an explosive reaction when mixed with Votras Alute." Zenna held her hand out, setting it on the floor in front of Malik. He hopped onto her palm, and she lifted him to her eyes. "You'll only have a few minutes before the blast."

"I thought you didn't make mistakes." Malik pecked her thumb in an affectionate gesture.

"Mother was experimenting. He wanted to increase the potency of Votras Alute. Instead, he nearly blew up the tower. Break a vial on the licorice root. As soon as the drug touches the plant, it will begin to smoke."

"Will the explosion be large enough to destroy the entire shipment?" Moira asked.

"It will be if Malik sprinkles licorice root throughout the room."

"Then, I shall expect you for dinner." Moira smiled. "Your parents will be excited to see you. They haven't stopped chirping since they arrived. Although I'm certain they would be happier to meet you in their human form, we'll correct that issue after you are safe."

"Who else was among the group I rescued?" Malik asked.

Moira's mouth folded into a thin line, her eyes sliding to Zenna as if she didn't want to reveal their names. "More than enough enemies to mount an attack against your father."

"What good will that do when they are all still birds?" Malik leapt off Zenna's hand and fluttered to the floor. "Are we going to peck him to death?"

"You will be human at sunset, as will the rest of them. I have enough powder to transform you all," Moira replied and disappeared.

"After I free Carlyle, I'll head straight for the west tower." Malik hopped onto the back of the mirror and snapped it shut. "Is there anything you want to take with you?"

Zenna nodded, rising from the floor. Stepping over him, she leaned across the bed, digging under her pillow. Pulling the necklace free, she lifted her hand. "Only this."

She tucked the necklace into her apron and walked to the curtain. Grasping the flimsy material with both hands, she yanked, ripping the curtain free of the thin rod running the length of the loft's entryway. She wadded the curtain into a ball and flung it down the staircase. It bounced off the last step and rebounded into the armoire, unfurling.

Zenna turned toward Malik. "Should I take the mirror, too?"

"We need to destroy it." He nudged the mirror forward. "Otherwise, my father can use it to find you."

As she leaned over and plucked the mirror from the floor, Malik hopped onto her shoulder, his little talons dug into her skin.

"Tired of flying?" she said, straightening, her mouth crooked.

"It's the only way I can touch you."

The familiar warmth of embarrassment flooded her face. She turned her head away from him and descended the staircase. Leaping over the curtain, she dropped the mirror on the sofa and headed for the wall of empty vials.

"There won't be much Votras Alute," she said, selecting the nearest vial.

"As long as he can walk, you can heal the rest of him after we escape."

It was as though she had plunged into ice water. Was this his plan all along, to destroy his father and take over the business? She froze and swallowed.

"You want me to make more?"

Malik scooted closer. "There are people who need this drug, people who are dying. Would you deny them?"

"I've spent my life in this tower, suffering at the hands of your father because of this drug."

"I'm not going to force you to do anything you don't want to." He sighed and nipped her ear. "I'm asking you to consider helping those who cannot help themselves."

"When did you become so compassionate?"

"When I fell in love with you." He bunted her jaw with his head, tickling her chin with his feathers. "However, before I can show you how much I love you, we need to get out of here."

She nodded, pulled the empty vial from the rack, and crossed the tower. Kneeling on the cold stone, she swept the residual powder into the vial, then held up the bottle, shaking it in the light. The vial was barely a quarter full.

"Is that enough?" Malik asked.

"Yes." Zenna capped the vial. Taking Malik gently from her shoulder, she flipped him upside down and placed him on her lap. After pulling a thread from the hem of her shirt, she wrapped the string around the vial and tied it to Malik's feet, then set him right-side up. "Can you fly?"

Malik flapped his wings, and his body lifted an inch from the floor. He dropped onto the ground, his feet resting on the vial. "I can manage."

"I'll give you three sticks of licorice root. Spread them across the floor of the western tower. You will need to shatter one vial on top of each root to ensure the powder reacts. The explosion should be large enough to break the other vials." She laid on the floor, bringing her eyes level with Malik. "You must be out of the tower before that happens."

"I will meet you in the center of the courtyard."

Zenna rose and darted to the back wall. Grabbing a jar, she unscrewed the lid and dumped the contents on her worktable. Sorting through the licorice roots, she selected three pieces of equal size and spun toward Malik. She took a deep breath to calm her racing heart.

Lifting Malik from the floor, she gave him a quick kiss on the top of his head and strode to the window, setting him and the licorice root on the windowsill. He scooped the sticks into his beak and turned back, his beady eyes finding Zenna. Nodding his head once, Malik leapt off the window ledge and soared toward the prison window.

She waited until she saw him land under the archway. Turning away from the window, she gathered the curtain from the floor and carried it to the sofa. She dropped onto the sofa and began shredding the curtain into strips.

"Why aren't you chained to the wall?" Mother's ire caused her to jump. She balled the strips together into a formless bundle and twisted around as Mother appeared beneath the staircase.

She gulped, her chest constricted. "I picked the lock."

"With what? I took—" A jar flew across the room, kicked by his boot, and shattered against the wall. The pungent smell of decay filled the room. He glanced down, his dark gaze sweeping over the remaining jars. "Why are these on the floor?"

"I was preparing for Malik. Did you bring him?" She shoved the curtain pieces into the sofa, and rose, clasping her hands in front of her waist. A flash of light zipped across the room.

Mother's gaze followed the glow to the mirror, resting on the sofa cushion, a peculiar smile pulling at the corner of his mouth. He strode across the room, shoved Zenna aside, and snatched the mirror from the cushion, prying open the clasp.

"Moira?"

13

"I'd like to say, it's a pleasure to see you again, Mac, but it's not." Moira's tight voice echoed around the tower.

"How is this possible?" Horror crept into Mother's face. "I watched you take your last breath."

"You always underestimated my skills." Moira clucked her tongue, and her voice dropped to a whisper. "You should have checked my pulse."

"Who helped you escape?" Mother's eyes bulged, and the hand gripping the mirror shook. "Was it Carlyle? I'll kill the son of a bitch!"

"No…" Moira dragged out the word, clearly enjoying Mother's vexation.

"Then, who?" Mother's anger vibrated off the rafters.

"The same person who told Malik I was still alive."

Darkness clouded Mother's eyes. "How long has Malik known?"

"About me?" Moira waited a beat. "Not long. Came as quite a shock to him, considering you described my murder to him in graphic detail on his fourteenth birthday." She paused again. "Where is my son?"

"I'd like to know the same thing."

"You would know better than I," Moira's tone hardened, "since you turned him into a bird, broke his wings, and threw him from a tower."

"Did a little waif tell you that?" Mother snarled, his dark gaze locking on Zenna. She took a step backward.

"I heard it from Malik's own beak," Moira replied.

"You've talked to Malik?" Mother paled, his gaze returning to the mirror.

"Several times. He introduced me to that sweet child you have trapped in the tower."

"She is not your concern."

"My son loves her." Moira's tone softened, flowing through the mirror, and wrapped around Zenna like a comforting blanket.

"He's a fool!" Mother's jaw clenched.

"Mac," Moira sighed his name as though this argument had occurred before. "I warned you not to stand in the way of his destiny."

"I taught him to take hold of his destiny."

"You taught him cruelty," Moira growled. "He will never be like you."

Mother's eyes narrowed. "How has he forgiven you so easily? All these years and you never came back for him. I would be livid."

"I was not strong enough to fight you, a feeling Malik understood quite well when I explained my position to him. Had I returned, you would have tortured and killed me in front of him. What good would I have been to my son dead?"

"You are no good to him now."

"It will be a pleasure to watch your world burn, Mac." Hatred flowed from Moira.

"It's been years. If you could hurt me, you would have done so already," Mother sneered, his lip curled.

"You're right, I can't touch you from here." Moira's voice hitched. "And I had to watch, every day, unable to intervene. The things you did to him…"

"So, this is your revenge, to blind my son with love." Mother slashed his arm at Zenna. "His infatuation will fade, just like every other girl he's met, and he will find a new amusement."

"I may have lent you most of my powers,"—Mother scoffed at Moira's words—"but divination was not one of them. Malik will take your kingdom with this girl by his side, my powers will be returned to me, and your punishment will be knowing I'm the one who brought about your downfall."

"Your son is dead." Mother snapped the mirror shut and threw it at the wall, where it shattered, flinging shards across the room.

Zenna screamed and ducked behind the sofa, her hands covering her face. Mother stomped toward her, his footsteps vibrated across the tower, stopped beside her head, and stooped.

"How many times did you speak with Moira?" Mother asked, his quiet tone sent ice sliding down her spine.

Zenna lifted her head, swallowing. "Once."

"What did you discuss?"

"The wedding." Zenna gulped as the lie left her lips. Would Mother believe her? She lowered her gaze to Mother's boots, fighting the urge to glance at the window. How much time had passed since Malik left? Surely, he would have freed Carlyle by now.

"The wedding?" Mother snorted and lifted her chin. A cloud passed across his face, and his eyes narrowed. "Did Moira tell you she had a vision?"

"I don't understand." Zenna pushed to a sitting position and frowned.

"Moira sees images, snatches of a potential future. Her talent was quite unreliable. She would go months without seeing anything, and even when she did, half the time, she got it wrong. Unless... she lied." Mother rose and paced the room, muttering to himself. Zenna's gaze followed his path, from the sofa to the window and back again. After three passes, he turned, his eyes landing on Zenna. "The only option is to relocate you."

A hard pit formed in Zenna's stomach. If Mother moved her before Malik caused the explosion, no one would ever find her again.

"You'll need time to regrow your hair, and that time shouldn't be interrupted with trivial distractions."

"Malik is dead, what other distraction would there be?" She climbed to her feet and wiped her palms on her apron.

"If Moira's vision has not corrected itself, then Malik must still be alive." Mother closed the distance between them. His hand whipped out and locked around her throat. "Where is he?"

"I don't know." She forced her tone to remain even, despite the frantic racing of her heart. "He's wherever you left him... You promised you'd let me save him."

"I assumed he succumbed to his injuries." Mother lowered his hand.

"Did you even look for him?" Zenna asked, wincing as she touched her fingers to the bruises forming along her neck.

"You can't produce any Votras Alute, so what would you do with a half-dead raven?" He arched an eyebrow.

"Escape! A prisoner has escaped!" Jax's voice rang through the compound. "Sound the alarm!"

Mother yanked a glowing mirror from his pocket. "Speak to me."

"Carlyle's gone." Jax paused. "As are all the birds."

"All the birds?" Mother's face purpled, and his anger rolled toward Zenna. "How did he manage to break loose from his chains, free the other prisoners, and escape with two broken legs, without anyone seeing him?"

"He had to have help," Jax replied, his gruff voice wavered, tinged with a whisper of fear. "Who would have turned against you?"

A motorcycle revved, the rumbling sound vibrating in Zenna's bones. Mother's gaze flicked to the window, his face darkened.

"Either you find him, or you take his place in irons."

"I'll bring him back."

"Alive!" Mother snapped the mirror shut and shoved it into his pocket. One thick finger stabbed Zenna's chest. "If I find out you had anything to do with this—"

"You'll kill me?" Zenna tilted her head. "How could I have helped him? I've been standing in front of you this whole time."

"Someone gave Carlyle a vial of Votras Alute, it's the only way he could have walked out of that prison." Mother's eyes narrowed.

"You took my hair,"—Zenna rubbed her hand over her bald head—"and the entire batch. How could I have healed him?"

Mother frowned, his frustration evident. "How did you intend to save Malik?"

"I was going to pull out my eyebrows. I'm not certain if it would work the same, but I hoped it would save his life."

"My prisoners escaped, Malik and Carlyle betrayed me, and a woman I thought was dead these past ten years suddenly reappeared, alive and well. The time has come to abandon this tower." He marched to her and wrapped his arm around her shoulders. One hand pushed her forehead back, forcing her to stare into his eyes. "We're leaving right now."

Her mind raced. She needed to stall Mother.

"Can I pack?" she asked and twisted her fingers together in an exaggerated nervous gesture.

"Pack?" Mother's brayed laughter echoed around the room. "What could you possibly want from this place?"

"It's been my home for twenty years," Zenna replied. "I'd like to say goodbye."

"As you wish." Mother waved his hand in a vague gesture. "You have five minutes."

"Thank you." She curtsied and ducked from beneath his arm, slipping out of reach. "Would you like to investigate the prison instead of waiting for me?"

"Jax has it covered," Mother said, a strange tone in his voice.

She nodded and walked to the armoire. Opening the door, she glanced back at Mother.

"Where are we going?"

"Why do you ask?" Mother leaned against the back of the sofa and folded his arms across his chest.

"I was hoping it would be near the beach, I miss the sound of the ocean." She pulled out a stack of white tank tops and was struck by the faint scent of Malik, whose unusual smell permeated the layers of cloth.

"You remember living near the ocean?" Incredulousness crept into Mother's question.

"Only the sound." She peeked at him over her shoulder. "I can hear it in my dreams."

"Unfortunately, that is not our destination."

"Will it be another tower?" She carried the stack of tank tops to the sofa and set them on the nearest cushion.

"Are you afraid of heights?" Mother asked, his eyes on Zenna.

"I would like the option to go outside."

"Is climbing on the roof not enough of an adventure for you?"

"I…" Zenna gasped and took a step back from the sofa.

"You seem surprised. Did you think I didn't know?" He leaned toward her. "I know everything that goes on in my compound."

"Except for what happened to Carlyle?" She should not have needled him, but the words slipped from her mouth before she could stop them.

Mother's arm flew, smacking her across the face. She stumbled backward, and Mother advanced, his eyes blazing.

"I think you know more about Carlyle's disappearance than you are telling me."

"I don't know what happened to him." She raised her arms into a defensive position, her gaze darting over the tower. There was no place to hide from Mother's anger.

"You will beg me for mercy long before we reach your new home." Mother lunged.

Zenna dodged him, turned, and darted up the staircase, running as fast as she could. She dove at the bed and landed in the center of the mattress. Mother appeared on the landing, his face a mixture of hatred and anger.

"Where is the curtain?" he growled.

A low groan echoed from beneath his feet. His eyes burst open, surprise filling them as the wood snapped, and one boot sank through the landing. He yanked his foot from the hole, lurching backward against the railing. The staircase shuddered, pulled away from the wall, and disintegrated in a cacophonic explosion. Mother disappeared in a cloud of dust billowing up from the pile of broken planks and coated the entire tower.

"Mother?" Zenna coughed. She crawled from the bed and inched toward the edge of the loft. Grabbing onto the wall, she peered down from her alcove, her gaze sorting through the jagged pieces of wood. Where was he?

She called him again, her tight voice was met with silence. There was not one whisper of movement below the loft. Was Mother unconscious or—she swallowed—dead?

Stepping away from the edge, she licked her lips. With Mother incapacitated—it was too much to hope he was deceased —she needed to fashion the rope as quickly as possible. She turned, her eyes skating over the tiny loft. The only thing of any use left up here was the small sack of food.

"Might as well take it with me." She murmured to herself and snagged it from under the pillow. Looping the string over her head, she turned back to the opening. Her hand dropped to the apron, patting the pocket to ensure her necklace was safely concealed.

The drop from the loft to the floor below was already significant enough to cause injury, Mother was a testament to that, but adding a pile of broken wood and nails to that landing made the feat even more dangerous. With both the quilt and the curtain on the sofa, she had nothing left to shred into a rope. She leaned over the edge.

"How am I supposed to get down?"

"I don't recommend jumping," Mother's gruff voice replied. One hand shot out of the pile of broken wood. Blood streamed down his arm, staining his skin crimson.

Zenna's stomach flipped over, tightening as her heart sped into a rapid pace, driving fear through her veins. She was out of time. She yanked the sack from her neck and flung it over her shoulder at the bed, and it landed with a soft thump.

Dragging his body from the wood, Mother clawed his way toward the sofa. When his legs were free of the pile, he flipped onto his back and stared up at Zenna, hatred glowed in his eyes.

"You caused this."

"I didn't do anything." She pressed against the side of the loft, partially hiding.

"Not directly," he groaned. His hand slid into his pocket and removed a vial. He popped out the stopper with his thumb, lifted his trembling hand to his mouth, and cursed. The vial was empty! Throwing it at the wall, it shattered, flinging glass and bits of deep purple powder across the tower.

"How is that possible?" Zenna mumbled to herself, her gaze dropped to the sparkling powder covering the broken staircase. She had seen the empty vial in Mother's hand.

"Moira!" Mother's voice vibrated with ire. A cackling laugh swirled into the tower, carried by a playful breeze that swept through the window and ruffled Zenna's hair.

Had Moira caused the staircase to collapse as well as turned the Votras Alute invisible? How powerful was she? Mother groaned, drawing Zenna's gaze. He shoved his fingertip into his mouth, sucking the deep purple residue from his thumb, and a shiver ran the length of his body. Forcing himself to a sitting position, Mother glowered at Zenna.

"You can't stay up there forever."

"How do you propose I get down?" she asked, her toes curling around the edge of the loft.

"Jump."

"Votras Alute will not save me."

"I will catch you."

"You're asking me to trust you?" Disbelief hovered in her throat.

"I'm telling you to jump before I transport myself up there and push you out of the loft."

Zenna nodded. Her eyes slid across the floor, seeking a spot free from debris. She took a deep breath, closed her eyelids, and stepped from the opening. Wind rushed past her ears as she fell. Her body tensed, anticipating the painful impact and sharp nails.

She crashed into something hard. Her eyes flew open. Mother, his chest heaving, stood in the center of the destroyed staircase, his arms wrapped around Zenna.

"You caught me," she gasped.

"I'm going to lose thousands while your hair grows back, and I'd prefer you alive for that process." Mother limped to the sofa and set her on the cushion.

"That's your own doing. You shaved my head." She glared at him. "You cannot add that loss to my debt."

"I can do whatever I want." Mother leaned forward and trailed his finger down her arm. "I own you."

An explosion rocked the tower.

Mother staggered and flung his arms out, struggling to keep his footing. Three tiles fell from the roof and shattered in succession behind the sofa, the pieces skipping across the stone floor.

Screaming, Zenna leapt from the sofa and ran, her arms covering her head, toward the window. She climbed onto the windowsill and spun around, planting her hands on both sides of the window. Her wide eyes locked on the roof. Four more tiles fell, surrounding Mother in a clay circle of sharp fragments.

"What the hell is going on around here?" Mother scowled at the rafters as if daring another tile to fall. After a moment, he turned and strode toward the window. Pushing Zenna aside, he leaned out and cursed, and Zenna twisted around.

Black smoke choked the sky, rising from—what Zenna assumed—was the west tower. She choked and covered her mouth with her arm. Climbing from the window ledge, she backed away from Mother, who vibrated with rage.

Malik had done it. The plan worked, except for one slight problem—Mother was still in the tower. He ripped the mirror from his pocket.

"Jax, where is Carlyle?"

"I can't find him, Boss. I lost his trail in the woods north of the compound."

"Get back here. There's been an explosion in the west tower!" Mother slammed the mirror shut. Twisting toward Zenna, his face tinged with the promised threat of agony. "Did you know?"

"No," she replied and took another step backward, her heart hammering. She knew Mother did not believe her lie. A black flash caught her attention, and her gaze shifted to the windowsill. She gasped.

Mother's eyes narrowed, and he spun around, a snarl curling his mouth.

"I should have known."

Malik cawed once, a taunt, and flapped his wings, hopping along the windowsill. Mother lunged, flinging his body halfway out the window. His thick fingers closed around Malik's tail feathers, just as Malik took flight.

"I am going to pluck every one of your feathers." Mother

grunted as he struggled to drag Malik back into the tower. "Then I'm going to stuff you a cage and hang you over my bed, so you're forced to listen to every ounce of pain I inflict upon Zenna."

"I won't allow you to hurt her anymore!" Malik twisted mid-air, ripping out his feathers. A horrific squawk echoed across the courtyard. When he sank his beak into Mother's hand, Mother howled and swung his other arm, his body precariously balanced on the window ledge.

"I win." Mother's fist closed around Malik.

"Let him go!" Zenna shouted and darted forward.

She grabbed Mother's arm, digging her heels into the stones, and yanked with all her strength. Mother jerked his arm free, wobbled, tottering forward, and flapped his hands, unable to regain his balance. His boots lifted from the floor, and he toppled, feet over his head, out the window, his hand clenched around Malik.

14

_____

"**M**alik!" Zenna screamed and flung herself at the window. Her hand stretched for Malik, her fingers brushing over his feathers. Mother flipped over mid-air, yanking Malik away from her, and tumbled toward the stone courtyard. Mother hit the ground with a deafening thud. His arms fell to the side, and his hand opened, releasing his grip on Malik.

Malik rolled out of Mother's palm and laid beside him, immobile. Blood trickled from Mother's mouth, dripping down the side of his face, pooled around his shoulder, and slid down a crack in the stone, racing toward the tower.

A small green vine poked up through the cracks, winding around Mother's legs, and wrapped around his torso, covering his body within seconds. A second thorn-covered vine pushed through the stones, crawling toward Malik's body, then a third and a fourth, until the ground beneath the tower was surrounded by a thicket of spikes.

"Malik!" Her strained voice carried across the compound. Tears leaked from her eyes. Malik was gone, buried underneath the thick vines.

She sank to the floor, her body shaking with sobs. Malik had sacrificed his life to protect her. He honored his promise. Mother would never hurt her again, except for the all-encompassing grief of Malik's death.

If she had been stronger or braver... Tears flowed down her cheeks, soaking her apron. Would Moira forgive her? Could she forgive herself?

Wiping her hand across her face, she rose and wobbled to the sofa on numb legs. She removed the curtain from the cushions and returned to the window, dropping to the floor. Shredding the curtain into strips, she laid them in a stack beside her, then fastened each end to the next, creating a long, thin rope. Malik's face floated into her mind, and a throbbing pain sliced through her heart.

"What the hell?" Jax's voice drifted into the tower.

Zenna popped up, brushed away the fresh tears, and glanced out the window. Jax stood in the center of the compound, his head swiveling between the burning west tower and the twenty-foot-wide thicket surrounding the south tower. In his hand, the mirror flashed.

"Mother won't answer you," Zenna cupped her hands around her mouth, yelling to Jax.

Confusion passing over the man's face, he marched over to the thorns and glared up at her.

"Where is he?"

"In there." She gestured at the thicket.

"What happened?" Jax took a step closer and reached out. He poked his finger, hissed, retracted his hand, and sucked on the tip of his finger.

"He fell from the tower," Zenna replied.

"Why are you up there?"

"It's better than being in the west tower." She offered him a smile. His eyes flicked to the fire raging to his right.

"Explosions, escaped prisoners, rapidly-growing thorns—if I

didn't know she was dead, I would suspect…" He shook his head. "It's impossible."

"Nothing is impossible, Jax." Carlyle's deep voice came from behind the south tower. He appeared, limping along the curve of the briar, and stopped beside Jax.

"Did you set the west tower ablaze?" Jax snarled, his hand dropping to the knife at his waist.

"No, I didn't, and there is no need for violence." Carlyle placed a heavy hand on Jax and squeezed his shoulder. "Your debt is cleared."

"Only Mother can do that." Jax glared at him.

"Or Mother's successor…" Carlyle shifted his gaze to Zenna. "Where's Malik?"

Zenna pointed down. "They're both in there."

Carlyle's eyes popped. He stepped toward the thicket, his path instantly blocked by giant thorns.

"Can you reach them?"

"I don't know." Zenna chewed her lip, she glanced down at the make-shift rope. Would it hold her?

"Malik would do the same for you," Carlyle's voice drifted through the window.

"He did more than that," Zenna murmured to herself.

She grabbed the curtain-rope, walked to the armoire, and tied an end around the leg, yanking it tight. As an added measure, she wrapped the end around the armoire's leg twice and flung the remainder of the make-shirt rope out the window.

"Is that safe?" Carlyle asked.

"Nope." Zenna climbed onto the windowsill, her gaze on the thicket. "Deep breath, Zenna."

She spun around and crouched down. Grabbing hold of the rope, she exhaled once, then slid out of the window, her fingers curling around the thin material. She climbed down the side, her feet planted against the side of the tower. Halfway down, the tension in the curtain eased. She glanced up. Fraying against the windowsill, one-quarter of the curtain's threads snapped.

"Hurry!" Carlyle's urgent warning echoed across the compound.

Dropping hand over hand, Zenna descended another ten feet before a horrific ripping sound vibrated through the courtyard. She screamed and fell backward, crashing through the middle of the thicket. Thorns carved up her back, shredding her skin to ribbons, then she landed with a grunt on a squishy surface. A groan echoed in her ear. Her heart squeezed, terror constricting her chest. How could Mother still be alive? She would never be free of him. A sob hovered in her throat.

"Zenna?" Surprise filled Malik's voice.

"Malik!" Her heart soared. She flipped over, ignoring the pain that accompanied the movement, and wrapped her arms around his torso, squeezing him with the exuberance racing through her body. He moaned. She released him, an apology on her tongue. Her forehead wrinkled. "When did you become a man?"

"Somewhere around the age of fourteen." His arms slid around her waist, and he drew her head down, brushing his lips over her mouth.

She pulled away. "I thought you couldn't transform—"

"Unless my father died." Malik tilted his head. "I don't think he survived the fall."

"And the thorns?"

"A little present from my mother to deter anyone who wanted to rescue my father."

"Miss?" Carlyle's voice floated through the bramble. "Are you alright?"

Placing her hands on his chest, she pushed up. "I found Malik!"

"Is he breathing?" Carlyle asked.

She glanced down at him and raised an eyebrow. "Are you breathing?"

"Barely, you're crushing my chest." She shifted, but Malik's arms tightened, pinning her against him. "It wasn't a complaint."

"He's alive!" she called back to Carlyle.

"I'll cut through the bramble from this side, but it will take some time. Crawl toward my voice." Slashing sounds followed Carlyle's command.

"What should I do?" Jax asked Carlyle, hesitance in his voice.

"Either grab a machete and help or leave, I don't care. You're free of your obligation." The thicket trembled as Carlyle slashed at the eye-level thorns.

"I need to find Katina."

The slashing sound paused. "She's safe with Moira."

"How is that possible?" Suspicion tainted Jax's question. "Moira is dead, and Mother said Katina was hidden where no one would ever find her."

"Katina was one of the exotic birds in Mother's collection. Malik freed her, along with Bear, and they flew to Moira's lodging, where she has hidden for the past ten years. I'll take you to her once we've recovered Malik," Carlyle replied and hit the bramble with his machete.

"Give me one of those." Swinging his arm, Jax sliced through the briar.

"We may have a bit of a problem," Malik said, drawing Zenna's attention from the conversation outside the thicket. He gestured at his leg.

Zenna turned, her gaze following his hand, and gasped. A long thorn, roughly one inch in diameter, stuck through his calf, blood oozing around the sides of the wound. She sucked in a quick breath.

"It's not as bad as it looked." He attempted a smile.

"I can break it off." She climbed off Malik, knelt at his side, wrapped her fingers around the thorn, and wrenched it sideways. Malik cried out, his torso jerking off the ground. She released the thorn, her hands flying to her mouth. "I'm sorry."

"Fine," Malik forced through his clenched jaw. He inhaled and exhaled, his chest moving slowly. A line of sweat broke out on his forehead. "It's too thick. You need something to cut through it."

"Mother's knife." Zenna's head whipped to the right. "He didn't fall far from where you stopped rolling. I'm sure I can find his body." She turned and crawled toward a small hole between the brambles.

"Zenna…"

"I'll be careful." She glanced back at him. "He might have some Votras Alute on him, too."

"I hate that stuff," he called after her, his voice waning as she squeezed through the thicket.

Thorns tore at her skin. She maneuvered around a large thorn, flattened her body to the ground, and slithered under a low-hanging branch. The sounds of Carlyle and Jax hacking at the thicket faded until the only noise accompanying her was the pounding of her heart. Mother could not have fallen this far from Malik.

She frowned, and turned around, catching her arm on a branch. Two long, thin lines appeared on her skin, carving scarlet trails from her shoulder to her wrist. She ripped a section from the bottom of her shirt and wrapped it around the deepest part of the cut. A scream echoed across the courtyard. Malik! Her heart constricted. She needed to find Mother fast.

Crawling in the opposite direction, her gaze scanned the dim briar, skipping back and forth over the shadows. Her eyes narrowed, stopping on a discolored portion of the bush. Boots! Scrambling over to them, she reached out and froze, her gaze flicked to Mother's chest. Had he moved?

She licked her lips and lowered her hand to his boot. She paused again, her nerves jangling, like a deer just before flight, and her blood pounded through her ears.

"You can do this," she said and rolled her shoulders back.

Lifting the boot, she yanked it from Mother's foot, and the

knife fell to the ground. Her hand whipped out, snatching the knife from beneath Mother's leg, and set his foot back down. She tucked the knife into her apron and crawled forward, sliding her hands up Mother's body. There had to be another vial, Mother always carried two on him. Her fingers closed around a solid cylinder in his breast pocket. Trembling, she pulled a small bottle from the pocket and inside sparkled Votras Alute. She tucked the vial beside the knife and turned away.

"Are you going to leave me here to die?" Mother asked. His gravel voice resonated with agony.

Zenna turned back, her body protesting, and terror rippled down her spine. It wasn't possible...

"Mother?"

"Give me the vial."

She cringed at his command, her body hunching over. Her hand dipped into the apron, closing around the vial, and her fingertips brushed against the cold silver of her necklace. Her head whipped up.

"No."

"No?" Mother snarled, his head twisting toward her, his eyes glowing black. Without warning, his body spasmed as if a bolt of lightning struck him. He screamed, his voice rising in volume as his body arched off the ground, then collapsed, unconscious.

"Mother?" Zenna scooted closer. She reached out and poked his chest. He gasped, his eyes flying open. His hand whipped out and closed around her wrist, dragging her closer.

"After everything I did for you, how can you let me suffer?" he asked, his voice tinged with agony, barely reached her ears. "I raised you."

"You kidnapped me. I don't owe you anything." She ripped her arm from his weakened grasp, turned away, and crawled toward the opening in the thicket.

"Have you no sympathy?"

Zenna froze. She glanced over her shoulder.

"Sympathy has no place in your business," she replied.

"My business," he snorted. "No matter what I did, I couldn't beat that horrible trait out of you." He coughed, and blood bubbled on his lips as his breath came in shallow gasps.

"I will ask your son what he thinks your fate should be."

"Malik survived?" Mother's head rolled toward her, surprised etched into his features.

"He did." Malik's deep voice came from behind her. He crawled through the opening on his elbows, dragging his legs behind him, and collapsed beside Zenna.

"How did you…"

"My father has been preparing me for that kind of pain my whole life." He lifted his head and grimaced. "You didn't come back. I was worried."

"I was held up." She retrieved the vial from her pocket and held it out to him.

"What did he want?" Malik growled, glaring at Mother.

"Compassion."

"A strange request from a man who has none." Malik pushed up on his forearms and took the vial. Popping open the top, he held Mother's gaze and tipped the vial, swallowing half the powder. He gagged and thrust the vial at Zenna. After a minute, he sat back and stretched his leg in front of him. Inspecting the injury, his eyes lifted to Zenna. "If I don't finish the vial, it will leave a scar."

"I don't mind your scars," Zenna said, her eyes on his.

"Are you asking me to spare his life?" Malik tapped the bottle against his chin. "To give compassion to someone who never showed it to either of us?"

"If you let him die, you're no better than him."

"He took your life!" Malik slashed his hand at Mother and growled. "Take revenge."

"I have." Zenna wrapped her fingers around his wrist and lowered his hand. "He will always owe me his life."

"I will only do it because you asked." Malik's gaze slid across the small area to his father. "If it were up to me, I'd leave you for the crows... I know you'd do the same to me."

Malik crept forward, the vial clutched in his hand. He stopped beside Mother's head and lifted it, setting it on his lap. Tipping the bottle, Malik tapped the remaining powder into his father's mouth.

Mother shuddered, his eyes closing, and he exhaled a long sigh. Opening his eyes, he shifted, rolling to his side with a grunt, and his dark gaze found Zenna.

"Stay with me, together we can rebuild this empire."

"I'll never work for you again," Zenna said, her voice calm. "My debt has long been repaid. I want nothing further to do with you."

Malik dropped Mother's head back on the ground and crawled toward Zenna.

"Carlyle will be through the briar before we return."

"I knew he was a traitor!" Mother sat up, his hands swirling a complicated pattern in front of his chest. Nothing happened. He repeated the action, a snarl curling his lip. Again nothing. Mother lifted his hands in front of his eyes and gasped. His fingers shriveled, his chalky skin stretched thin, displaying a grim outline of his bones. "What the hell?"

"She warned you," Malik spoke quietly, his back to his father. "You stole what wasn't yours and used your gift to hurt people. You've been found unworthy of the powers lent to you. She took them back. The amount of Votras Alute coursing through your body may have restarted your heart after you died, but the suffering you are about to endure will be much worse than anything you've ever done to one of your victims." Malik turned around and stared at his father, an unreadable expression flowing across his face. "You have a great number of enemies, many who spent the past several years as birds, trapped in small iron cages beneath the compound. They will stand against you... with me."

Turning away, Malik jerked his head, indicating for Zenna to head toward Carlyle. She nodded and ducked under a low bramble. As she crawled forward, a low growl stopped her heart. She spun around just as Mother lunged for Malik. In Mother's hand, glittered a small dagger. He sank it into Malik's side. Malik collapsed.

Zenna screamed, scrambling toward them. Mother raised the knife again and slashed toward Malik's heart. Zenna dove forward, knocking Mother's arm aside. The knife flew from his hand and buried itself between two rocks.

"It's too late." Mother laughed, his gruff voice sent ice sliding down her spine. "You can't save him now."

"I spared your life," she gasped, her eyes locked on the red stain forming on Malik's shirt.

"I told you, sympathy has no place in my business." Leaning forward, Mother grabbed Zenna's wrist and dragged her toward him. "We'll have no more of these foolish romantic notions, we're going back into business."

"No." Malik forced the word through his lips. His fingers closed around Zenna's ankle as Mother yanked her through the thicket.

Mother jerked Zenna free of Malik's feeble grasp and snarled, "Tell your mother, I'll see her in hell."

The thicket exploded, shooting brambles twenty feet into the air. Zenna covered her head with her arms as thorns rained down, encompassing the clearing. A wall of spikes blocked Mother's path.

"Tell me yourself."

The air beside Mother shimmered as Moira appeared. Before Mother could react, she bent over, ripped the knife from the stone, and smashed it into his heart. Releasing Zenna, Mother glanced down at his chest, paling. He grabbed the knife handle and slumped over, exhaling one final breath.

Zenna scrambled over to Malik. Blood leaked from his

159

abdomen, pooling beneath his body. She pressed her hands against his side. Malik lifted his arm, his fingers closing around her wrist. Zenna lifted her gaze to Moira.

"Can you help him?"

"Of course, child." She smiled. Kneeling beside Zenna, she placed one hand on Zenna's shoulder and one on Malik's.

The air vibrated, the thicket blurring until it became a whirling cyclone of tan. Zenna felt as though she had been jerked from the ground and flung through the air. Malik's hand tightened around hers as they spun faster. Zenna squeezed her eyes shut, bile rising into her throat. They stopped suddenly and collapsed onto something soft.

Zenna peeled one eye open and stared at the ceiling of a cavern. Light flickered across the smooth grey rocks, lit by iron torches lining the walls.

"Where are we?" she asked, her soft voice echoing as she sat up.

"In the northern mountain range," Moira replied. She glided past the bed, heading for a giant fireplace carved into the side of the cave. She lifted a ladle from a giant cauldron swinging over a fire. After pouring the steaming liquid into a silver goblet, she returned to the bed and held out the cup. "He needs to drink all of it."

Zenna nodded, accepting the goblet. "When can I see my parents?"

"I have one more errand to attend before I reunite you with them." Moira placed a hand on Zenna's arm, and squeezed. "They are overjoyed to meet you, dear child. Your mother has been pacing her chamber since she transformed back into her human self. I just need a bit more time to ensure we are all safe."

"What are you going to do?" Zenna asked.

"I'm going to burn Mac's compound to the ground." Moira's face darkened. She waved her arm and vanished.

Malik groaned, his eyes fluttered open. "Did we make it?"

"Almost. Drink this." Zenna lifted his head, placed the goblet to his lips, and poured the liquid down his throat.

"It takes like hair." He coughed, choking on the liquid.

"Your mother made it."

"Then it's definitely hair." He grinned as horror crossed Zenna's face.

"I thought I was the only one who…"

"You are." Malik took her hand and brought it to his lips. "She has a small stock of the dried flower that originally created Votras Alute, enough to heal those my father injured."

"Will you be alright?" Zenna's gaze dropped to his abdomen.

"Would you like to inspect the wound?" Malik lifted the blood-stained shirt, revealing a fading scar. She reached out and touched his stomach, trailing her fingers lightly over his skin. He trembled and sucked in a quick breath. His hand closed around hers, desire pooled in his eyes. "When will my mother return?"

"As soon as she burns down the compound." Zenna glanced down at her hand, where his thumb traced a light pattern over the back of her skin. "I can't believe it's over."

"He's never coming back for you."

She lifted her eyes to his. "What do I do now?"

"You could marry me." He wiggled his eyebrows. "I've been told the ocean is an ideal locale."

"Malik…" She bit her lip. Mother's warning ricocheted in her mind. Was she merely a passing amusement? "There's no obligation between us."

"You don't want to marry me?" He tilted his head.

"Your reputation…"

"Is wrong." His fingers tightened. Dragging her arm forward, he pulled her on top of him, and his mouth brushed against her lips. Tingles zipped through her limbs, and her stomach clenched with need. His tongue pushed into her mouth, sliding along hers and stealing her breath. Wrapping around her body, his arms crushed her against his chest.

She broke away panting. Taking a deep breath, she exhaled slowly, slowing her heart.

"I think your reputation is fairly accurate."

"Zenna,"—he cupped her face, his eyes searched hers—"I'm in love with you, no matter what my father said. I never thought happily ever after was a possibility for someone like me. I'm not going anywhere,"—a wicked smile pulled at his mouth—"and I'm going to enjoy using all of my experience to make you scream my name over and over again."

Heat flared in her cheeks.

"Before my mother brings my uncle, your parents, and everyone else my father has wronged in this room, I'd like the opportunity to hear your sweet voice call my name at least once." He grinned, drew her face to his, and pressed a soft kiss to her lips.

EPILOGUE

"Are you certain you don't want to grow it out?" Anna asked as she sank down on a long sofa beside Zenna and drew her fingers through Zenna's short hair.

"I like this length." Zenna tugged on the strands, barely even with her jaw. Her eyes slid to a curtain dangling over the entrance to the cavernous room—one of several extending off the cave's main room. On cue, Malik pushed the cloth aside and entered.

"As do I," he said and held up the curtain for Enzo and Moira to pass through.

"I spent twenty years as a bird," Enzo said over his shoulder to Moira. "Every time I look in a mirror, I expect to see bright green."

"Mac is gone," Moira said, patting Malik on the shoulder as she passed him. "You have nothing to fear from him or anyone else. My magic will prevent anyone from changing you into a different form."

"So, I'm human forever?"

"As long as you live," Moira replied and shrugged. "I cannot prevent death."

"Zenna could." Malik moved out from behind them and stole across the room. He sat on the opposite side of Zenna and drew her hand to his mouth, pressing a light kiss to her knuckles.

Moira shook her head. "Votras Alute cannot cure death. Mac's heart stopped when he fell from the tower, and the drug restarted it, but it did not prevent him from losing all the powers that were loaned to him, nor did it prevent him bleeding to death after I stabbed him."

"Are you certain he's gone?" Anna asked. Her voice wavered.

"I watched his body burn," Moira replied. She shifted her attention to Malik and nodded to him. He slid from the sofa and dropped to the floor beside Zenna, her hand still in his.

"As I am no longer a bird, and you are no longer a prisoner, there's something I'd like to ask you." He reached into his pocket and extracted a small, silver ring. "Zenna—"

"Rapunzel."

"What?" Malik's head whipped toward Anna.

"We named her Rapunzel when she was born." Anna forced a tight smile. "Mac changed it to Zenna after he took her."

"Rapunzel." The word rolled across Malik's tongue, drawing a faint blush to Zenna's cheeks. He grinned. "From the moment I climbed into your tower, I could think of nothing but stealing you away, and now that you're free, you have a decision to make. Nothing would give me greater pleasure than to marry you... if you would have me."

"There is no other person I would rather live happily ever after with than you." Zenna slid from the sofa, landing in Malik's lap, and he slid the ring onto her finger. Leaning her head against his, she slipped her arms around his neck, and pressed her mouth to his.

Moira, Anna, and Enzo exited the room, but neither Zenna nor Malik noticed. Wrapping her in his arms, Malik lifted Zenna from the ground and carried her to the bed. He set her on the mattress, covering her body with his. His hand slid down her waist and closed around the long skirt of her dress, drawing it up her legs.

"I much preferred you in my shirt," he murmured against her lips.

"Me, too." She wriggled against him, impatience coursing through her veins.

His mouth curved against hers. "I am going to enjoy undressing you, though, over and over again."

The End

Thank you for reading *Hair, She Bears.* If you enjoyed this twisted fairytale, please leave a review wherever you purchased the story, it really does make a difference. If you are interested in learning more about new releases, behind-the-scenes author secrets, sales, and giveaways, sign up for my newsletter.

NEXT, I invite you to take a peek into another twisted fairytale of mine, CURSED (Paranormal Tales, #2). To save her childhood crush from an amphibian fate, a waitress strikes a fool's bargain with a slighted enchantress.

♥Alyssa

CURSED

"I will give you the chance to save Kaleb."

"To save Kaleb from what?" Rana swallowed, glancing at the mouth of the alley, hoping someone would walk past.

"Eternal damnation."

Rana's head whipped back to Celeste. "He doesn't deserve that."

Celeste tapped her finger on her chin, considering Rana's comment. "You believe he has merit?"

"Yes."

"Would you be willing to stake your life on that?"

Rana gulped, trying to determine if Celeste was dangerous or simply crazy. "What would I have to do?"

Celeste grinned. "Merely agree to take his place."

"As in, allow you to kill me?"

"Certainly not." Celeste laughed, the mirthless sound echoed down the alley. "That was an emotion-driven episode. You have nothing to fear from me during your test."

"My test? What do you mean?"

"You just need to perform one little task. Nothing illegal," clarified Celeste, answering Rana's unasked question. "Once that is complete, I will forgive Kaleb's slight."

"And keep your business arrangement with Mr. Prince."

Celeste tilted her head, her olive eyes glowed. "Aren't you an intriguing one... Agreed, as long as Mr. Prince *wishes* to do business with me."

Waving her arm, Celeste drew a burning blue symbol in the air. It glowed brightly, pulsating. Words hissed from Celeste's mouth in a mysterious language. The symbol flashed, flying straight at Rana's chest, and vanishing. A golden hourglass appeared at Rana's feet.

"You have until sunrise before the spell becomes permanent. I suggest you hop to it."

"Wait a minute, what do you mean by *spell*?"

Celeste's maniacal laughter echoed down the alley as blackness poured into Rana's mind, drowning her. She collapsed. Shadows marched across the mouth of the alleyway, brushing over Rana's unconscious body, and hiding her in their inky darkness. Beside her head, sand flowed through the golden hourglass.

The End

Cursed – Revenge is a dish best served green.

ABOUT THE AUTHOR

USA Today Bestselling Author Alyssa Drake has been creating stories since she could hold a crayon, preferring to construct her own bedtime tales instead of reading the titles in her bookshelves. A multi-genre author, Alyssa currently writes Historical romance, Paranormal romance, Contemporary romance, and Romantic suspense. She thoroughly enjoys strong heroines and often laughs aloud when imagining conversations between her characters.

She believes everyone is motivated by love of someone or something. One of her favorite diversions is fabricating stories about strangers surrounding her on public transportation. When she's not whipping up chocolate treats in the kitchen, Alyssa can often be found madly scribbling notes on a train or daydreaming out the window as the scenery whips past.

http://www.alyssadrakenovels.com

Read More from Alyssa Drake

AVALISSE ROSS MYSTERIES
(co-written with Bella Emy)

VIRTUALLY YOURS (book 1)
ETERNALLY YOURS (book 2)

~

DAMSELS DEFEATING DISTRESS

FORTRESS OF DESIRE
HARBOR OF SECRETS
SHELTER OF INNOCENCE
Published as part of *With Love from Dublin*

~

DARK TALES FROM FIREFLY ISLAND

AFFLICTED
DEVOURED
ELECTRIFIED
PETRIFIED (free)
SCORCHED

~

PARANORMAL TALES FROM FIREFLY ISLAND

CONJURED
CURSED
DAMNED
(Coming soon)
HEXED
POSSESSED
SUMMONED

~

THE WILTSHIRE CHRONICLES

AN IMPERFECT BARGAIN (free)
A PERFECT PLAN (book 1)
AN IMPERFECT ENGAGEMENT (book 2)
A PERFECT DECEPTION (book 3)
AN IMPERFECT SCOUNDREL (book 4)
(Coming soon)

Made in the USA
Middletown, DE
02 December 2021

54058241R00104